"YOU ☙ W9-AXD-872

Prudence spat the words at him. "You horrid, evil man. This is blackmail."

"Yes, I suppose it is. But then, there is not a very pretty word for what you have been doing either, my dear," sneered the comte.

"I never kept any of those jewels!" she exclaimed in a whisper. "Any money I . . . acquired . . . went for a truly noble cause."

"I see there is no false modesty in the Pennhallow family," he murmured. "But come now. We are straying far from the subject. The Lansing ball is coming up next week."

"No!" she gasped.

"Oh, yes. I realize her ladyship will most likely wear the famous Lansing rubies, but she has a diamond necklace that is almost as famous."

Prudence stared at him in horror. "The Lansing diamonds," she exclaimed. "I could not."

"Oh, but I think you could . . . to avoid bringing scandal upon your family. What would the ladies of the ton say if they were to discover that one of their brightest jewels was nothing more than a common thief?"

Not to mention Lord Brimley, Prudence thought with dismay . . .

❈❈❈

THE LIGHT-FINGERED LADY

THE
LIGHT-FINGERED
LADY

Sheila Rabe

Naper —
Lovin' ya Bunches!
Sheila

PAGEANT BOOKS

Publisher's Note: This is a work of fiction. The characters, incidents, and dialogues are products of the author's imagination and are not to be construed as real. Any resemblance to actual events or persons, living or dead, is entirely coincidental.

PAGEANT BOOKS
225 Park Avenue South
New York, New York 10003

Copyright © 1989 by Sheila Rabe

All rights reserved. The right to reproduce this book or portions thereof in any form must be obtained in writing from the Permissions Department of the publisher.

PAGEANT and colophon are trademarks of the publisher

Cover artwork by Hector Garrido

Printed in the U.S.A.

First Pageant Books printing: January, 1989

10 9 8 7 6 5 4 3 2 1

To Mom, always a lady

Chapter One

Lady Ashby's ball was, like all her parties, a smashing success. And because it was rumored that Prinny himself would be putting in an appearance, the only members of the ton not present were either sick or dead.

The hostess beamed at her guests as she circulated among the crowd. She would sleep well tonight, having again proved to herself and the world at large that she was the undisputed center of London Society. This ball had been an expensive form of proof, but old Ashby was rich as Croesus and everyone knew he never begrudged her a farthing.

"A delightful affair, my dear," one of her cronies said. "But it looks as if one of your guests may have had too much of a good thing." She

1

pointed with her fan to the dance floor, where a young woman obviously overcome from exertion was being led away from the dancing throng.

"Oh, dear," muttered Lady Ashby, "the Pennhallow child."

"Quite," murmured her friend, smiling.

"And wouldn't you know Louisa chose tonight of all nights to be home with a megrem," complained Lady Ashby. "I tell you this, Esmerelda, I think the child overindulged. I am sure these dizzy spells are all in her mind. And I, for one, don't intend to spend my evening hovering over her with sal volatile. She will either recover or go home."

With this declaration Lady Ashby made her way across the room to where Miss Prudence Pennhallow was now enthroned in a chair. Her dance partner had left in search of punch and two other young swains had taken his place. She looked up into their concerned faces with big blue eyes. A listless hand brushed a golden ringlet from her damp forehead and she smiled . . . weakly. She sighed and said, "I am fine, truly. Only, Lord Alvaney, please let me cry off for the quadrille. I think if I can just rest for a few minutes I will be fine."

"Say you will recover in time for the waltz you promised me and I'll willingly forgive the quadrille," said the young lord. "And as for Smythe here, consider it a blessing if you're not well enough to dance with him. For I have never known a man to make such a career of treading on toes."

"Oh, pooh!" said Miss Pennhallow with a

laugh, temporarily forgetting her weakened condition. "Mr. Smythe is a delightful dancer and I do so hope we will have a chance to stand up together later."

Lady Ashby had come within earshot in time to hear this speech. Her thin lips compressed in a line of disapproval. Silly young clouts, she thought. The girl was a heartless flirt. "Dear Miss Pennhallow," she said, forcing concern into her voice as she barged her way into the conversation, "are you not feeling quite the thing?"

"Oh, Lady Ashby, I am fine!" declared the frail Miss Pennhallow. "I was a little dizzy, but I'm feeling much better now." Then, as if speech had weakened her, the young woman fell back against the chair. A small hand pressed against her heart and she sighed.

Lady Ashby eyed her young guest, who was lying back on the chair, her blond curls in charming disarray, with a mixture of emotions. She was sure the girl was no more sick than herself. But, on the other hand, she did not want the chit to faint on the dance floor and make a public display. Not with Prinny due any minute! Lady Ashby was not about to let her moment of glory be eclipsed by a young miss in her second season. "You really do not look well, my dear. I think we should send for your carriage."

"Oh, no! Then Constance would have to leave and she's having such a wonderful time. I would hate to spoil the evening for her."

Fortunately for Miss Prudence Pennhallow, her hostess did not look to see for herself whether Constance was having a good time. For if Pru-

dence's sister was having fun she had an odd way
of showing it. Her smiles were fleeting and
whenever the movement of the dance permitted
she cast a worried glance in her sister's direction.

"Your aunt only allowed you to come without
her tonight because she is my dear friend and
knew she could count on me to watch over
you," said Lady Ashby. "She charged me with
your care and if something were to happen to
you . . ."

"If I could just lie down for a few moments I
would be fine," Prudence assured her.

"Come then, my dear," said Lady Ashby, anxious to be done with the nuisance. "Let me take
you to my room. A few moments' peace may be
all you need." And with that she bustled Miss
Pennhallow out of the room and off to her bedchamber.

"I am so sorry to be a bother," said Prudence as
the strains of the music grew softer and Lady
Ashby's pace quickened.

"Nonsense," lied the good lady. " 'Tis no
bother. Here we are." She opened the bedroom
door and ushered Prudence into a room full of
knickknacks and frills in every imaginable shade
of pink. Prudence blinked at the papered walls,
swimming with pink roses. If she hadn't been
dizzy before she surely would be if she had to
stare at those walls for very long. Every piece of
furniture in the room was upholstered in some
shade of pink, but the most commanding by far
was the bed, shrouded in pink gauze and covered
with a dusty-rose coverlet.

Knowing what was expected of her, Prudence

managed an expression of delight. "What a lovely room!" she exclaimed.

"Thank you," said a beaming Lady Ashby as she led Prudence to the daybed. "I do think pink is such a restful color." Her ladyship procured a small vial from her crowded dressing table and pressed it into Prudence's hand. "If you should feel the least bit faint, do not hesitate to use this." She sat on the couch next to her patient. "Now tell me," she commanded, "does your head ache?"

Prudence shook her head. "Dear Lady Ashby. You are kindness itself. But I have detained you from your guests too long. You must not feel you need sit with me, especially when you are expecting such an important guest at any moment."

This reminder put the lady on her feet in a hurry. "I do hope you will be well enough to join us soon, my dear. I'll send my abigail to check on you in a little while."

"Thank you," murmured Prudence as she subsided among the pillows.

The door closed and Prudence began to count slowly. Upon reaching ten she made a remarkable recovery and jumped up from her sickbed. She remained standing for a moment, listening intently for any sounds outside the room. Hearing none, she tiptoed to the door. She cracked it open and peered out. Satisfied there was no one in the hall, she shut the door and again surveyed the room.

Her eye spotted her quarry almost instantly and she ran to the dressing table where sat a large, carved wooden box inlaid with silver. She opened it and her eyes were dazzled by the wink and sparkle of the gems inside. Prudence bit her lip in glee. "Well, dear Lady Peacock, which of your feathers would you not miss?" She pulled out a diamond bracelet and held it up. It was simple in design—rather boring, really. Only diamonds, and small ones at that. But valuable, nonetheless. "I think you've outgrown this in taste as well as size," Prudence told her absent hostess. She bent quickly and, pulling up her gown, hooked the bracelet above a shapely ankle. She stood for a moment with her skirt still lifted and twisted her foot, admiring her prize. The gems twinkled up at her. "I thank you, milady," she whispered, "and my orphans thank you." The skirt fell into place and Prudence, completely recovered, tripped from the room and made her way back to the ball.

Guests were just taking their places for a set of country dances when Prudence reappeared in the doorway, a vision in pale blue. The honorable Mr. Smythe, the second son of a very rich and powerful Whig family, was anxiously looking about. His ruddy face broke into a smile when he saw her. "Here, Miss Pennhallow!" he exclaimed, nearly trampling a plump matron in his effort to reach her. "Dare I hope you are recovered enough to stand up with me?"

"Yes, sir," Prudence said and dimpled at him. "I believe you may so dare."

"Capital! I am glad to see you're feeling better."

"Yes. It is a most remarkable recovery, is it not?"

"I don't wish to seem forward, Miss Pennhallow, but don't you think you should see a doctor about these spells? If I remember correctly, you had one only a fortnight ago."

"Oh, a doctor would just think me a silly female who imagines herself ill. No. It is something I seem to have inherited from my mother. I believe she was prone to dizzy spells when she was young. I am sure this is something I shall outgrow as well."

"Well," said Mr. Smythe, obviously not convinced, "it still seems to me you should see a doctor. There ain't nearly enough pretty girls in London and I, for one, should hate to see anything happen to one of the prettiest."

"A very charming speech, sir," said Prudence with a laugh. "And what nonsense! There are many girls in London as pretty as I—and with more than just good looks to recommend them—and well we both know it."

Mr. Smythe was not offended by this unmaidenly statement. He and Prudence were old friends, he being one of her favorite admirers last season until her engagement removed her from the ton's selection of eligible females. He gallantly insisted that fortune wasn't everything and his dance partner laughingly argued that many of their friends might disagree with that.

"I already have all the blunt I need," said Mr. Smythe.

"What an unfilial statement," said Prudence laughingly. "I am sure your mama and papa would not like to hear such talk. I think I should tell them."

Mr. Smythe's eyes bulged. "You wouldn't!"

"I might," threatened Prudence, giggling.

Mr. Smythe shook his head at his tormentor, who dimpled up at him and batted long eyelashes in a most entrancing way. She continued to tease her gullible partner and so the dance passed pleasantly and Mr. Smythe returned his fair companion to her seat feeling honored to have been so teased by the lovely Miss Pennhallow.

Remembering she had supposedly been feeling ill less than an hour ago, Prudence assumed an attitude of fatigue and begged her next partner to allow her to sit out their dance. She had no sooner dispatched him in search of refreshment than a pretty girl with light brown hair and eyes as blue as her own snatched the vacant seat next to her. "What have you been about?" the girl hissed behind her fan.

"Nothing, dearest. Are you enjoying yourself? I see Lord Wentworth is becoming most particular with his attentions."

"Don't change the subject," said Constance, her voice rising. She blushed and lowered it to a whisper. "Have you been up to what I think you have?"

Prudence lowered her eyes demurely as her admirer approached with her punch. "We can talk about it later, dear. Do go have a good time."

"How can I have fun, may I ask, when I'm walking in fear that my sister may end on the gallows?"

"Don't be a ninnyhammer," Prudence commanded in a quick undertone. "Ah, thank you, sir. I am sure this will revive me. Oh, Constance, here comes Lord Wentworth to claim his dance."

Constance squinted in the direction her sister had pointed. A smile lit her face and her eyes opened wide as Lord Wentworth came into focus.

"Enjoy yourself, love. I'm sure I'll see you at supper," said Prudence sweetly.

This kind benediction brought wrinkles to Miss Constance Pennhallow's brow, but she allowed herself to be led away with only one backward pleading look to her sister.

The sisters did not meet again until the evening's end, when they were to leave. In spite of small dowries they were both exceptionally pretty, and were kept busy dancing.

Prudence, in fact, was more than exceptionally pretty. She was considered a Diamond of the First Water and fortunate to have been blessed with the fair coloring so currently popular as well as an assurance and liveliness many young ladies lacked, and of which their mamas disapproved.

Constance did not possess the remarkable beauty of her older sister, but there were many gentlemen who considered her lovely despite her squint. After all, the poor thing couldn't help it if she was as blind as a bat. And once a gentleman got within full view of Constance, the squint left and he was treated to a lovely sight—a pretty face with large blue eyes and a sweet smile.

It was to be expected such charming girls would be popular. Only when safely inside their carriage did they have a chance to speak privately.

"Well?" demanded Constance as the carriage moved slowly down Park Street.

For an answer her sister lifted her skirt and stuck out a prettily shod foot. There on her ankle the diamonds glinted in the moonlight.

Constance gasped. Then she fell back against the squabs and moaned, "We're ruined. This time you'll be caught for certain. I know it."

"That is what you said last time," said Prudence with a laugh, "and here we are, safe and sound. Lady Ashby will never miss this. The fat old peahen has a dozen like it."

"Oh, Prudence, it is wrong and you know it."

"No, it's not!" exclaimed Prudence. "This will go to a certain establishment tomorrow and be turned into money—money which will feed a good many orphans, children who are barely existing while we dine on lobster patties and fancy ices," she finished in disgust.

Constance sighed and began a lecture that had become all too familiar to her sister. "Dearest. This is not Sherwood Forest. It is London. And you are not Robin Hood. You are Prudence Pennhallow, a girl from a good family . . ."

"With no dowry because her father squandered most of his fortune," Prudence finished. "Papa's conduct is merely another example of how our class selfishly squanders its wealth."

Constance looked shocked.

"I am sorry," said Prudence, taking her hand. "I don't mean to sound ungrateful. You know I love Papa as much as you. But he has brought us to a sad pass. Sometimes I wonder how we manage to scrape by."

Constance said nothing. What could she say? Her sister was right. Their reckless parent was a lovable but irresponsible man who had done great harm to the family fortune by the affair he started with Lady Luck after his wife's death. He spent most of his time with his cronies at his club or at Crockford's, parting with his money while he waited for his luck to turn.

"What Papa needs," said Prudence, suddenly inspired "is a new interest to take his mind off gambling. A new wife!" she exclaimed.

Constance, temporarily diverted, laughed. "Oh yes, a lady of birth and fortune who would like to marry a pudgy old gambler."

"A *charming,* pudgy old gambler," her sister corrected. "I am sure somewhere in the ton there is a woman for him. We are going to have to pry Papa away from his cronies and induce him to come with us to more of these affairs."

"Cupid himself could not accomplish that," said Constance. "Besides, suppose we got him to a ball? He'd get no farther than the card room. No. I think we shall have to settle for finding rich, indulgent husbands. For you are right. *Someone* is going to have to keep Papa. Oh, Prudence!" Constance exclaimed in exasperation. "We have strayed far from the subject at hand. Please, dearest. No more of these mad adventures. You are sure to be caught." Prudence made no reply. "Oh, I think something has come unhinged in your brain!" declared Constance, exasperated.

Prudence laughed. "Nothing has come unhinged, I assure you. And all will be fine. You'll see."

Chapter Two

There was a certain jeweler in Cranbourne Alley known as Hamlet who enjoyed the patronage of the ton when they found themselves in financial difficulties. Whist, faro, and hazard often proved to be an irresistible temptation and the early morning hours saw many a gentleman creep round to Hamlet's establishment to pledge his inherited gold and silver plate or his wife's diamonds for a cash loan. Sometimes Hamlet saw females as well, for many of the ladies were as addicted to gambling as their lords. Often, after the gentlemen had left, the little man could be seen ushering a veiled lady into the room at the back of his shop.

Prudence had learned of this unusual jeweler from her Aunt Louisa at the beginning of the season. Auntie had been crowing over the misfortunes of an old rival who was temporarily reduced to trading in some of her best pieces for paste imitations. "Arabella Ashby's brother saw her carriage parked not ten feet from old Hamlet's only yesterday. Cranbourne Alley! Imagine! A fine place for a lady."

Aunt Louisa's timing couldn't have been better, for her niece had just successfully completed her first jewel heist and at that very moment had a hot necklace sitting in her reticule.

Fortunately, Aunt Louisa unwittingly supplied the needed information and Prudence had gone to see Hamlet immediately, taking a terrified Constance with her. The carriage was left a discreet distance from the shop and the two veiled ladies entered with all the bravery of a fly approaching a spider's web.

Prudence's hand had shaken when she produced the necklace she wished to sell—a modest piece made up of garnets—and the little man looked sadly at her. "So young to be having difficulties," he murmured to his assistant, and gave her more money than he normally would have.

Prudence had left with a fat purse and a light heart and had wasted no time in championing a cause that she had longed to aid ever since her previous London season. Again, Aunt Louisa had been an unknowing tool, having once taken Prudence with her to visit the Edgar Timms Home for Orphaned Children, always in need of money. It was one of Aunt Louisa's favorite charities and her niece's heart was instantly captured by the wistful-looking little faces that had peeped at her from over the banister.

Prudence had longed to help those poor orphans and provide them with every possible creature comfort. Unfortunately, her pockets and those of her family were sadly to let. But most members of her class had more than enough. And a chance remark of her sister's had given her a brilliant idea. If Robin Hood could rob from the selfish rich and give to the poor, she reasoned, why couldn't Prudence Pennhallow? With her usual enthusiasm and only a small amount of serious consideration, Prudence had plunged into a most satisfying adventure.

Taking from the rich had been an easy task. And giving to the poor had proved most rewarding.

Mr. Biddle, the administrator, had been overjoyed by the sudden appearance of such a lovely and generous patroness and he had been greatly impressed by her desire to have her gifts remain anonymous, thinking this request sprang from humility. In truth it sprang from fear of being found out. The fat little man had assured Miss Pennhallow that her wish would be respected and thanked her profusely—all the way to her carriage.

So Miss Pennhallow's great adventure had begun. The previous night's theft had been her third and she now considered herself quite expert. Her hand no longer shook when she laid out her treasure for Hamlet's inspection. And she walked bravely into his establishment, no longer fearing the unknown. She went alone, taking only James the footman. And she left him waiting discreetly at the carriage while she conducted her business with Hamlet.

This was fine with Constance. It had been all well and good to laugh about what fun it would be to play a modern-day Robin Hood, but the situation had gotten out of control. Who could have imagined her sister would really do such a thing? Now she had—and not just once, but three times! "I can only hope," Constance said the morning after Lady Ashby's ball, "that you will soon find some man to distract you from this dangerous pastime."

Prudence looked down her nose at her sister and in her most affected voice said, "Oh, yes. I couldn't agree with you more, my dear."

Constance glowered at her sister, who broke into peals of laughter. She tried to retain her stern look but finally was forced into a reluctant smile.

"That's better," said her sister. "Really, dearest, you're not a dowager yet."

"I feel old," sighed Constance.

"Do stop worrying so. I've done this three times now and everything has gone perfectly."

"Then I suppose it is about time something went wrong," predicted the sage.

"Nonsense. I've gotten quite good at this. No one is going to catch me," Prudence assured her, pulling on her gloves. "After all," she added, "this is my second season and I do know how to take care of myself. If Auntie asks where I am, tell her I took my pearls to get the catch repaired. I shall give your regards to Mr. Biddle."

"Do try and be back before Auntie wakes up," begged Constance. "You know I have never been able to deceive her—she is far too sharp for me."

"You could get up and come with me," suggested Prudence.

"I thank you, no," Constance replied, shuddering. "Cranbourne Alley quite oversets my nerves."

"I never thought you would turn into such a pudding heart! Very well, I shall hurry." Prudence blew her sister a kiss and left her to her worrying and her hot chocolate.

*   *   *

While Prudence was busy playing Lady Bountiful there was great excitement in another part of Mayfair. In one particular town house in Arlington Street the lovely Angella, Lady Farnsworth, was receiving a surprise visit from her brother, Lord Brimley.

"Eddie!" she squealed, and, mindless of her exalted position, jumped from her chair and rushed to him. "I thought I had misheard when Remley announced you."

The gentleman laughed and bent down so she could kiss his cheek. "Most unladylike, m'dear," he said. "One would think you hadn't seen me in years."

"Well, it certainly seems that way," retorted his sister, tossing her dark curls. "You hole yourself up in the country too much."

"Precisely," agreed Brimley.

"And furthermore . . ." she began. Angella blinked. "Beg pardon?" she said.

"So you should," replied her brother, easing himself into a chair and taking a glass from the tray Remley proffered. "My compliments to old Foxy," he said after sipping its contents. "Your husband has excellent taste. A new acquisition?"

"I believe so," said Angella, leaning back against the sofa and fixing her brother with a quizzical glance. Obviously, he was in the mood to play games. Well, she would wait him out.

Edward Chatsworth Oswald, the Earl of Brimley, flicked a speck from his jacket and said casually, "I've tired of the country."

"If they still dress like that," said his sister, eyeing his attire, "I should think you would be."

Brimley looked ruefully at his garb. His jacket had looked fine enough at his country seat, but here in town he was conscious of its inferior cut. The rest of his wardrobe was in no better shape. He tugged at his shirt collar in an unconscious effort to raise the shirt points. "I do intend to remedy this, Angel. I am making a visit to Weston this afternoon, and I shall be seeing Hoby tomorrow. After all, I'll have little enough time to myself once word gets out I am in the market for a wife."

"A wife?" repeated his sister stupidly.

"Come now, Angel. You never used to be so slow. What has happened to you?"

Brimley's sister could have retorted that it was only natural she should be shocked. After all, her brother had been a widower for over five years.

Brimley's period of mourning hadn't been extended indefinitely because of a broken heart. His had been a marriage of convenience. The dowry had been sizable, his mama thought the girl sweet, and society thought her a Beauty. With the encouragement of his mother, who was anxious to see her only son well settled, he had rushed to declare himself, married as soon as possible. The couple had dealt well enough together for two years until his wife's death in a hunting accident. Although the marriage had not been a bitter failure, he and his wife had had little in common and had often spent weeks occupied with their separate interests at opposite ends of the house.

After her death he had vowed never again to let himself be tricked by a pretty face or bullied by his family into a life of domestic boredom. He had finally buried himself at his country seat, immersing himself in business affairs and the running of his estate.

His mama, when she was still alive, had tried to lure him out of retirement, as had his sister, but to no avail.

But that was five years ago and Brimley was tired of his solitary existence, so after years of dodging every trap set by the matchmaking mamas of the ton as well as his female relations, he was ready to voluntarily put his foot in a parson's mousetrap. Small wonder his sister gaped at him.

"Well, what do you think?" asked her brother. "Once I am properly rigged out I should be considered quite a catch."

"You shall be quite a catch no matter how you dress and well you know it," answered Angella. "But why this sudden desire to marry?"

"I'm bored," complained the earl.

"You were bored when you were married," Angella reminded him, cocking an amused eyebrow.

"Yes, but this time I shall choose more wisely."

"You are a man so I doubt you shall do that."

"What, pray, does that mean?" demanded Brimley.

"It means exactly what you think," replied his sister. "Men rarely choose wisely. After all, what need have they to do so? Wives take up so little of their time, really. We are merely ornaments or the means by which they may acquire an heir."

"I have never felt that way!" exclaimed her brother, shocked out of his cynical posturing.

Angella ignored him. "A husband, however, is a different matter. And a woman must choose wisely, for her future happiness is very much at stake."

Brimley had considered his sister happily married the last two years. Her speech was lightly delivered, but he couldn't help wondering if some discontent had prompted her remarks. He eyed her seriously for a moment until, as though reading his mind, she laughed and said, "Why the glum look? I have chosen well and fared better than many of my friends who are neglected by their husbands. Foxy prefers the card room to the ballroom, but I am not so old that I lack other partners. He is kind and indulgent. What more could I want?"

Brimley eyed his sister dubiously, but politely changed the subject. "Then Farnsworth can have no objection to my squiring you about?"

"I am sure he would prefer you to some of my other cicisbei," Angella said with a laugh. "But I shan't be seen with you until you do something about your clothes."

"Never fear," said Brimley. "Have I yet given you reason to blush?"

"Many times, dear. But never for your looks," said Angella. "If you think you can be transformed by Tuesday next you may take me to Almack's."

"How that particular tradition has managed to endure is beyond me," he grumbled.

"It has endured because it works very well," answered his sister. "Come now, you want to see what's available, don't you?" she coaxed.

"I should prefer to see what's available at a ball or a small dinner party."

"I shall give you your very own dinner party," promised Angella, smiling. "And if you are nice to me I may even give you a ball."

"How kind," Brimley murmured.

"But," she continued, ignoring his impertinence, "you may as well go to Almack's first." She uncrossed her legs and planted them on the floor, a hand on each knee. "Look 'em over first, old fellow—see what there is to choose from," she said gruffly.

Brimley laughed. "Gad, but you are an impertinent chit. And you make a terrible man."

"I think I should have made a splendid man!" exclaimed Angella.

Her brother shook his head. "You are still a minx. Well," he said, standing up, "Almack's it shall be. In the meantime, see if you can get it about that I am in town."

"You will be swamped with invitations before the week is out," Angella predicted. "Oh, but this will be fun!"

Chapter Three

By the following Tuesday Lord Brimley had been transformed from a dusty rustic to a smart-looking man about town. His sister observed his attire and smiled her satisfaction. There would be no reason to blush for the cut of his coat now. Its lines proclaimed the workmanship of a smart London tailor. His cravat was intricately tied, its white folds setting off his tanned face and handsome, dark features. His black evening breeches fit just as they should, showing off the muscular thighs of a man in top physical condition. "Well, Eddie," she declared, "what a difference a new set of togs make! You will quite outshine every other gentleman at Almack's tonight."

Brimley bowed. "I think I'll do," he said.

"You certainly shall," agreed Angella. "We shall be positively besieged with matchmaking mamas!"

"I have already been besieged," Brimley informed her as they made their way down the stairs and out to the waiting carriage. "Do you know I have already been invited to three balls, five routs, and seven dinner parties? I had forgotten how exhausting a London season can be."

Angella giggled. "Don't let it fret you. Country life has obviously kept you in fine physical condition. I am sure you will have no problem bearing up under the rigors of town life."

21

Almack's was already crowded by the time Angella and her handsome escort arrived. Middle-aged mamas doted over fresh-faced daughters decked out in white or pastels with every imaginable embellishment to enhance their femininity, from knots of ribbon to pearl rosettes. And the girls came in every size and color.

"Well?" asked Angella as Brimley handed her a cup of lemonade. "There's Miss Sorenson, in the pink. A nice-sized dowry, I understand."

"Too plump."

"Miss Ingleson?"

Lord Brimley wrinkled his nose. "Too thin. Really, Angel, have you no taste? Who is that?" he asked, nodding in the direction of a pretty little brunette with thick-lashed brown eyes and a small rosebud mouth.

"Miss Elyza Lansing. Quite a sweet thing."

"Lansing chit, eh. Quite a fortune, then."

"Every season must have an heiress. It does make for entertainment, watching all the gentlemen scramble for her favors."

"And who is that scrambling now?" asked Brimley, looking at the slim, elegant gentleman chatting intensely with Miss Lansing.

"The Honorable—and I use the term loosely—Thomas Daltry. A bit of a loose screw from what one hears. I believe Lady Lansing and his late mother were dear friends in their youth. I cannot imagine any other reason why he would be allowed to dangle after the girl. Everyone knows Daltry's father has gambled away half the family fortune and mismanaged what little is left. Daltry is hunting for an heiress."

"The lady obviously doesn't mind."

"The lady is a pea goose."

Just then Prudence danced into view. "And who is that?" demanded Brimley.

"That is Prudence Pennhallow. Good ton but no money." Lady Farnsworth eyed her brother. "I see Troy is again about to fall because of a lovely face."

Brimley caught the mischievous glint in her eye and reflected it back. "Never mind the history lesson. Tell me what you know of this fair Helen."

"Not a lot. But enough." Angella looked speculatively at her brother, then said, "Why don't you try the Lansing girl. She's much more conventional."

"Minx! You are egging me on," said Brimley. "Come now. I have already risen to the bait. Let me take it."

His sister laughed. "Very well. But don't say I didn't warn you. As I said, I don't know the family well. She seems a nice enough girl. And she and her sister have very pretty manners. But there is something odd about her."

"Intriguing. Do go on."

"The girl is either clumsy or accident prone. I have not yet decided which. She has twice this season managed to get her skirt torn under some poor gentleman's foot. And the latest on-dit is the dizzy spells. She seems to have them quite often and has set it about that they run in the family."

"And that is all? Really, Angel. You disappoint

me. For a moment I thought there was something really odd about her."

"I think there is," insisted Angella.

"Sounds like a storm in a teacup to me," commented her brother. "And a storm brewed by some jealous woman at that."

Angella ignored this comment and took a sip of her lemonade. "I see Lady Sorenson about to descend upon us with the lovely Miss Seraphina," she said. "Really, Eddie, I do not think her too plump."

"Never mind Miss Sorenson," he ordered. "Tell me more about Miss Pennhallow before they pounce on us."

"There's not much else to tell. It is her second season and her sister has just come out this year."

"Second season? How did such a Diamond get through a season unclaimed?"

"She didn't. Old Edgewood offered for her. But he died before he could claim his bride."

This casual comment caused her brother to open his eyes wide. "The girl *does* seem to be unlucky, doesn't she? Nevertheless, I expect you to introduce me after I've done the pretty with little Miss Sorenson here."

"I shall, on one condition."

"What is that?"

"You must promise to watch your feet when you are dancing with her," said Angella with a giggle.

Lord Brimley did his duty and danced with Miss Sorenson. When he returned her to her mama there was another woman waiting to present her daughter to him. The girl, an insipid thing with thin lips and a long nose, just happened to have the next dance free. Lord Brimley gallantly begged her to allow him the chance to lead her into the next set. Once rid of her he found two more ladies waiting with blushing maidens in tow.

And so the evening continued. Brimley shot his sister as many pleading looks as he could, but she perversely chose not to understand and merely nodded and smiled. Finally, however, her conscience was pricked and she came to rescue him. He had just returned a very plump damsel to her mama and was mopping his damp brow, smiling politely at the two matrons elbowing each other in front of him. One was just reaching out a hand to grab his arm when his sister came up beside him and tugged him away, saying, "Dear ladies, I know my brother will ring a peal over my head for dragging him away from such fair company, but I have someone waiting who has been dying to make his acquaintance all evening."

"Well!" exclaimed one woman to the other as Angella swooped off with their prey. "Haven't we all?"

Actually, Prudence had been far too busy enjoying herself to spare too much time worrying about how to make the acquaintance of the handsome stranger in Almack's. She did, of course, notice him. Who wouldn't notice that intriguing, dark face, with its wide brow and piercing brown eyes. The gentleman was so tall that he stood well above the heads of most other men in the room.

"It's Lord Brimley," Miss Lansing informed her

as the two young women watched Lady Farnsworth and her brother from across the room. "He is quite dashing, isn't he, Miss Pennhallow? Although he is awfully large. It quite frightens me the way he looms over one when one is dancing."

Prudence thought she wouldn't mind being loomed over by the earl, but she didn't allow such an unladylike thought to be put into words. Instead she merely smiled and nodded, waiting to see if her new friend had gleaned any other interesting bits of information about the newcomer.

"I danced with him already this evening and he was quite nice but not nearly as considerate as Mr. Daltry," Miss Lansing continued. Prudence frowned at this statement. It was Miss Lansing's first season and the poor thing was very green. Prudence was about to give her a sisterly warning about the notorious Mr. Daltry when the girl exclaimed, "Oh, my, here comes Lord Brimley! I think I will go see if Mama wants something to drink." And with that she scurried off, leaving Prudence to face the giant alone.

"Miss Pennhallow," said Angella, "pray don't think me too forward. I hope you will allow me to introduce my brother, Lord Brimley, to you. He has only recently arrived from the country and is sadly out of touch with society. And at this moment he lacks a dance partner."

All during this speech the giant had stood silent. Now he came alive. "I have been in the country most of these last five years, but I think I won't disgrace you, Miss Pennhallow, if you will allow me this dance."

For one who had been hidden in the country, his lordship looked exceedingly fashionable, Prudence thought. His frilled shirt, coat, and breeches were all that was proper, and his muscular calves were encased in as elegant a pair of silk stockings as Prudence had ever seen. As for his lordship's abilities on the dance floor, Prudence had caught a glimpse of him there and had been amazed at the grace with which he maneuvered his large frame. "I would be delighted, sir," she said simply.

"I could ask you how you are enjoying your stay in London," Prudence said as he led her onto the floor. "But I am sure you've been asked that so many times this evening you are already tiring of your visit to town—or at least your visit to Almack's."

"You are a most perceptive young lady," said Brimley, smiling.

"Oh, not perceptive," she said, and smiled back. "But not insipid either."

At that Brimley laughed. "Miss Pennhallow, I can see why it has taken most of the evening to arrange a meeting with you. No wonder you are so in demand. Tell me," he asked when the movement of the dance allowed, "are you of the Leicestershire Pennhallows?"

"The very same," she replied.

Brimley nodded and smile politely. He had heard of the family. The father was rather a loose screw, a hearty fellow, always eager to place a bet and, from what one heard, more than happy to allow his widowed sister to rule his roost. Rumor had it Pennhallow had barely a feather to fly with.

"Very pretty country," Brimley said diplomatically.

"Oh yes!" agreed Prudence. "I think it is some of the prettiest country in all of England. Although I haven't traveled much," she admitted. "Only to London. But I can't imagine any place prettier." She smiled at Lord Brimley. "Do you suppose I have not much imagination?"

His lordship returned the smile, warmed by the lady's quick wit and her ability to laugh at herself. "I suspect," he replied, "it is more a case of loyalty to happy childhood memories than lack of imagination."

"How very chivalrous!" exclaimed Prudence. "My lord, I can see you are very diplomatic and I predict you will soon be the most popular man in London. I feel fortunate that I can now number myself among your acquaintance."

"I must say, Miss Pennhallow, I feel equally fortunate to have met you," he replied.

The dance went on and Brimley and Prudence maintained a flow of small talk throughout, Miss Pennhallow unknowingly making more of an impression on the earl with each passing minute. Not only was she beautiful and clever, observed Brimley, but she also possessed a refreshing frankness. It was this frank and open manner of speaking that made her stand out from the other young ladies he had danced with, who studied every word for its possible effect on him before letting it out of their mouths. He also noticed she did not toss her curls like the accomplished flirts or look artfully up at him from under those thick eyelashes. Instead she looked him straight in the eye and smiled as if they were old friends. Here was an unusual young woman to be sure!

When the musicians scraped to a halt it was obvious neither Lord Brimley nor Miss Pennhallow had any desire to end the conversation. Their progress back to her aunt was a slow, pleasant journey. But once Prudence was returned his lordship was again besieged and captured by yet another scheming mama and Prudence saw him no more that evening.

At dawn, as the Pennhallow carriage threaded its way through Almack's departing throng, Aunt Louisa narrowed her watery blue eyes and scrutinized her niece. "I must say you and Brimley made a prodigious handsome couple."

"Oh, Auntie," said Prudence laughingly. "Looking well together doesn't count for much."

Aunt Louisa lowered her head, giving herself three chins, and eyed Prudence. "No. However, getting along well does. And I noticed you were getting along very well indeed."

Feeling slightly uneasy at the flow of the conversation, remembering how her aunt had bullied her into an engagement last season, Prudence changed the subject.

"Did you not see old Dudley making sheep's eyes at you tonight, Aunt?"

On that comment both girls looked accusingly at their aunt.

Lady Burton blushed and began to fan herself as though the carriage had become suddenly hot. "Really! You two girls are becoming quite insolent. What would your poor mama say?"

"She would ask you why you don't get busy

and bring old Dudley up to scratch," replied Prudence, and the girls began to giggle again.

"Lord Dudley to you, miss," corrected Aunt Louisa, trying to look formidable. "Anyway, why would an old woman like me want to disrupt an already perfectly comfortable life by marrying?"

Prudence turned to Constance in mock horror. "Our aunt is trifling with that poor man's affections!"

The sisters began to giggle again and Aunt Louisa grimaced. Both her charges were in high spirits and there was obviously no getting them to settle down and talk seriously this night. She heaved the sigh of a martyr.

In another coach, Lord Brimley and his sister were also discussing the evening. "And how did you find the assembly, Eddie?" asked Angella.

"Much as I remember, though I do believe the girls have gotten younger and more shallow. Every young lady I danced with either quaked like a blancmange in my presence or agreed with every word I said. And they all seemed to say the same things—as if they'd been coached."

Angella laughed. "Of course they have, silly! They all must catch husbands and their mamas cannot have them saying things which will put a gentleman off."

Brimley frowned in disgust.

"And the fair Miss Pennhallow, how did you find her?" his sister asked in an arch tone of voice.

"Far from fainting," replied her brother. "She seems a most robust young woman."

"Ah, looks can be deceiving," Angella reminded him.

"Yes, they can," he agreed, remembering his first wife. How she had charmed him the one time he had met her before he had made an offer! Her beauty had promised such rapture, such happiness. But he had discovered, to his disappointment, that beauty wasn't worth much when you wanted to play a decent game of whist on a cold winter's night or share a joke. How the laughter died out of a joke when you had to explain it! Brimley dragged his mind from the past and refocused it on Miss Pennhallow. "The girl entertains me. Does she attend all the tedious affairs this season?"

"I see no reason why she would not."

Brimley twirled his quizzing glass and smiled. "It may prove to be an interesting season yet."

His sister grinned and shook her head at him. "It may at that," she agreed. Brimley was obviously intrigued by Miss Pennhallow, and something told Angella that that young lady would lead her brother a merry dance. Well, once Edward set his mind on something there was no stopping him. She could only hope that this time his impetuous heart would not lead him too far astray from the happiness he deserved.

Chapter Four

As soon as word spread through society that he had returned to London, Lord Brimley was nearly buried alive under a pile of gilt-edged invitations. He picked up a handful and sighed. Brimley considered himself as sociable as the next man, but the mere thought of enduring a London season exhausted him. He sifted through the cards, remembering his sister's careful instructions on which invitations he might politely decline and whose he must, on no account, refuse. He toyed with the idea of discarding Lady Sorenson's card. He had met the lady at Almack's and she struck him as an exceedingly silly woman. But, if his sister was to be believed, she was one of the ton's leading hostesses. "Best not," he muttered. "Angel would be furious." However, he did weed out several invitations that he could safely decline and after disposing of them he felt better able to face the social rigors of the next two weeks. He then strolled off in the direction of Gentleman Jackson's boxing school to get himself in shape for Lady Sorenson's upcoming ball.

The Pennhallow ladies were also preparing for the ball. The merits of investing in new gowns as opposed to disguising old ones were discussed. It was finally decided that for this particular occasion some clever needlework would serve just as well as a visit to Fanchon's. "I think we can do it!" Prudence exclaimed, shutting *La Belle Assemblée* and setting down paper and pen.

"Yes," agreed Constance, "but I wish we didn't have to."

"I know, dearest. This scrimping and scratching certainly isn't what Mama would have wished for us."

"I am sure Papa doesn't wish it either," said Constance.

Prudence smiled and shook her head. "No. He would be horrified if he knew how economical we are. But we must be a little practical. We cannot have Aunt Louisa always outfitting us, even though she loves to do it. And how horrid it would be to have Papa dunned on our account! Anyhow, I fancy before the year is out you will be Lady Wentworth. And then you will have any number of dashing new gowns."

"Do you really think so?" asked Constance.

"I know so!" exclaimed Prudence. "Really, love, the way he looks at you—anyone could tell he is quite besotted."

"His mama is nice also," said Constance, her blue eyes turning dreamy.

"Yes, you shall all deal famously together."

"Prudence—" ventured her sister. "You hadn't planned on *doing* anything at the Sorensons' ball, had you?"

"Nothing that would hurt your chances of snaring Wentworth, love," her sister assured her.

Constance smiled, relieved. "Now I can look forward to the ball with an easy mind," she said.

Her sister smiled at her with the face of an angel.

* * *

A week later the sisters joined the glittering
throng at Sorenson House, where the ballroom
was even more crowded than the Ashbys' had
been. Lord Wentworth, however, easily spotted
Constance and appeared by her side as soon as
she entered the room. He had already extracted a
promise for the first dance as well as the privilege
of escorting her down to supper. Now he begged
a waltz of her as well and bore her off to greet his
mama before the dancing started.

Aunt Louisa spied an old crony and pulled Prudence off with her until she should be claimed.
Her niece had just settled herself into a chair and
arranged her skirt when a tall form cast a shadow
over her.

"Good evening, Miss Pennhallow," said a deep
voice. "Dare I hope you have this dance free?"

Prudence wished she did, but she saw her
friend Mr. Smythe bearing down on her. "I am
afraid not, my lord," she said with regret.

"Perhaps another."

"I think so," she replied as her partner arrived.
Duty-bound, she presented Smythe to the earl.
The two men exchanged polite bows before Mr.
Smythe led her out to the floor.

"Dashed handsome chap," said Mr. Smythe,
studying Prudence's face.

Prudence smiled at her friend. "Yes, he is," she
admitted. "But beauty isn't everything, is it?"

"No, come to think of it, it isn't," Mr. Smythe
cheerfully agreed, and led his partner onto the
floor.

Prudence was a picture of grace as she danced

with the clumsy Mr. Smythe. And she looked lighter than air waltzing with Lord Alvaney. But later that evening when it came time to dance with Lord Brimley she seemed to lose her powers of concentration. How it happened he never knew, but she managed to get her skirt under his lordship's foot. There was a ripping sound and Brimley looked down in amazement to see that her gown was no longer in one piece. A portion of flounce was hanging sadly down.

For the first time since he was a youth Brimley felt a blush creep over his face.

"Oh, how careless of me!" exclaimed his partner.

"I don't know how I could have been so clumsy," Brimley apologized.

"No, my lord, it was me. I was not attending to what I was doing." Seeing the embarrassed look on his face, Prudence felt suddenly guilty. She could have, after all, used Mr. Smythe. He was notoriously awkward. But that would have been very unkind, and the evening was passing swiftly. She could ill afford to delay any longer. Lord Brimley could spare a moment's embarrassment for a worthy cause. "It is only a small tear and easily mended," she assured him. "Do let us finish this dance. I promise to be more careful and keep my gown out from underfoot."

Brimley agreed. But the rest of the dance was far from enjoyable as he spent it concentrating more on his feet than his partner. He was relieved when it ended and he could return Miss Pennhallow to her aunt. "I am afraid I don't bring her back in the same condition as when I took her away," he confessed.

Aunt Louisa raised an eyebrow and Prudence laughed. "I got my gown in Lord Brimley's way. It is a wonder I didn't trip the poor man."

"I think I have been away in the country too long," said the earl, shaking his head.

Aunt Louisa chuckled. "Our Prudence seems accident prone this season. Pray, don't worry over such a trifle as a torn flounce."

"Thank you." Brimley turned to Prudence. "Please let me know if the gown turns out to be beyond repair."

"Really, it is only a small tear," said Prudence. "I will just pin it up and it will be good as new." Then, excusing herself, she sought her hostess's daughter.

Upon seeing the damage, Miss Sorenson exclaimed, "Oh, what a pity! It is such a lovely gown."

"I think it can be mended," Prudence assured her. "I have some pins with me and if I may use your sitting room I'll just pin it up and it will be fine."

"Of course," said Miss Sorenson. "I shall send Rose to you. Oh, dear, here is Mr. Smythe, come to claim his dance."

"I wouldn't dream of keeping you!" exclaimed Prudence. "Mr. Smythe would never forgive me. I am quite sure I can find my way."

"I should go with you . . ." said Miss Sorenson doubtfully. "Mama would wish me to."

"But I should hate to see you miss a dance. Mr. Smythe is quite sweet, isn't he?"

"Oh yes," agreed Miss Sorenson, a betraying flush spreading across her round face. "And such an elegant dancer."

Prudence smiled at this—love *must* be blind! "Do not worry about me. I shall manage just fine."

Miss Sorenson finally gave in. "Very well," she said, beaming at Mr. Smythe. "It is the second room on the right."

"Are you unwell, Miss Pennhallow?" asked Mr. Smythe, concerned.

"No," said Prudence. "Only very clumsy. I have managed to tear my gown."

"Well, thank God it wasn't me who stepped on it!" exclaimed Mr. Smythe.

Prudence laughed and left him to the ample charms of Miss Sorenson.

By a process of elimination she found Lady Sorenson's sitting room. Its soft colors were restful and, unlike Lady Ashby's, bid the entrant stay. However, Prudence hadn't the time. She quickly picked the lock on her hostess's jewel box with a hairpin and rummaged through the treasure trove. It took only seconds to find the perfect piece—a ruby ring stuffed in a corner. This should do, she thought. She plunked the treasure into her reticule and quickly pinned up her gown. Then she opened the bedroom door and stepped out into the hall. She gave her gown a shake and, satisfied that her flounce would remain attached for the rest of the evening, left, leaving the room only slightly emptier than when she had found it.

She returned in time to be claimed for the next dance.

Lord Brimley watched her from the side of the room, curious. There was something strange about Miss Pennhallow; his sister was right. Yet he wished he could get to know her better. He sensed something kind and intelligent beneath her careless manner; something altogether different from the usual debutante. Supper would be served after this dance and, much as he liked his sister, he would have preferred taking supper with the intriguing, accident-prone Miss Pennhallow.

Angella, standing next to her handsome brother, noticed the casual glances cast in that lady's direction. "I am glad you are only my brother. Otherwise I should be quite jealous."

He looked at her under lazy lids and smiled slowly. "I suppose you think yourself very clever. Just remember, men don't like women who are too clever."

"I needn't worry about that anymore, need I? I'm married," retorted Angella.

"Poor Farnsworth."

"And how fares the lady's flounce?" asked Angella.

Brimley shook his head. "Odd. I've never in my life done such a thing. I can't think how it happened."

"I can tell you how it happened," said his sister. "The lady very gracefully laid her gown under your foot."

"Ridiculous!" snapped Brimley.

"Ridiculous but true, nonetheless," replied

Angella calmly. "Doubt me if your vanity demands it."

"What reason would she have to do such a thing?" Brimley asked after a moment's silence.

"Heaven knows. But it appears obvious Miss Pennhallow needed a torn flounce. And you were her tool."

Brimley was disconcerted by his sister's remarks. Could it be true? He watched Miss Pennhallow. She was listening intently to her companion, her upturned face frank and honest. Was that the face of a deceptive woman? Brimley shook his head. "No, Angel. You must be mistaken."

"Eddie, I tell you I am not," insisted Angella, following his gaze. "The girl is up to something, I'll wager." Angella smiled. "I do wonder what it is."

Chapter Five

After she had been helped out of her evening finery Constance came to her sister's chamber for their customary bedtime chat. Prudence had purloined the last of the plum cake from the kitchen and the girls climbed into her bed to eat it, subsiding in a billow of blankets. "I do think you may be right about Lord Wentworth. He seemed most particular in his attentions tonight," Constance said, licking a finger, a dreamy look on her face.

"I told you so. He is a very good catch and I am happy for you." Prudence smiled at her sister. "If I weren't so happy for you I could almost be jealous, you fortunate girl. You will be marrying for love and money."

"Maybe you will, too," said Constance gently.

"I should certainly like to," sighed Prudence. "But if I cannot marry for love, I shall at least marry for friendship. Last season was a close call —it taught me that a girl must be practical and consider more than her family's wishes or the size of her suitor's pocketbook. I shall at least like the man I marry."

Prudence drew the covers more tightly around her. "I certainly don't want my husband to be as old as Lord Edgewood was. He did try hard to be sweet, but oh, dear, he was *so* wrinkled—even his lips!" Prudence shuddered. "Imagine being kissed by him. It would have been like kissing a prune!" She laughed at the look of distaste on her sister's pretty face. "Well, you shall suffer no such fate. Lord Wentworth is so charming and handsome. And he has merry eyes. I could tell before I even met him that he likes to laugh. I think you shall suit."

"Yes," Constance agreed. "I think so, too. Do you know, I feel almost sorry for girls like Miss Lansing."

Prudence looked perplexed.

"Take us, for example," explained Constance. "We know our suitors like us because we're, well, us. Everyone knows we aren't rich. But poor Miss

Lansing. How does she know if her suitors are attracted to her or to her fortune."

"You are right, dearest," said Prudence. "But I don't think Miss Lansing gives the matter any thought at all. She is too busy enjoying her season."

"Of course, that makes her rather vulnerable, does it not?" put in Constance.

Prudence nodded. "Yes, but fortunately she has her papa and mama. I am sure they will watch over her carefully."

"Well," said Constance doubtfully. "You had Papa and Aunt Louisa and look what almost happened to you."

"Oh, my, you are right!" said Prudence slowly, her eyes opening wide. "We had best keep an eye on her."

Constance nodded agreement, and then, having safely ensured their new friend's future, returned to the subject nearest her heart. "Lord Wentworth is so kind. And such an excellent dancer." She hugged her knees and smiled. "I had a wonderful time tonight. I am so very glad you did not do anything foolish. Although you did give me an uneasy moment when your flounce was torn. But since you promised you wouldn't . . ." Constance's voice trailed off. Her sister was wearing the same look she used to wear when as children they were caught in some wrongdoing and she wanted Mama to believe them innocent. "Prudence. Say you didn't!" Constance demanded.

"Didn't what?" asked Prudence, turning wide eyes upon her.

"Prudence, you promised!"

"I promised I would do nothing to hurt your chances with Lord Wentworth," said Prudence. "And I haven't!"

"Did you steal something from Lady Sorenson tonight?" Constance demanded.

"Only a small ruby ring."

"Prudence," Constance moaned. "You will ruin us all."

"Oh, stuff! Really, Constance. Mrs. Siddons is most fortunate you are ineligible for a career on the stage, for you would quite outshine even that famous actress, carrying on so . . ."

"About nothing," he sister finished for her. "Of course it is nothing, so if you should happen to get caught . . ."

"I won't!"

"And what," said Constance, trying a different approach, "if Lady Sorenson should discover her ring missing and accuse her maid of taking it? The girl would be turned off without a reference. But I suppose that is nothing to concern us."

"Of course it is!" exclaimed Prudence. "If Lady Sorenson turns off her maid we shall hire her. But really, don't you think you are letting your imagination run away with you? I am only taking the smallest of trinkets which these greedy ladies will never miss."

"Greed is exactly why they will miss the jewels," Constance argued. "I am sure they check from time to time to make sure no one's hand has been dipping into their jewel boxes. And even if they don't discover anything missing, someone is bound to catch you in the act eventually. Someone will notice your suspicious behavior and figure out what you are up to."

"Bah!" exclaimed Prudence. "You call my behavior suspicious only because you know what I am about. To anyone else a torn flounce is merely an accident and a dizzy spell could happen to any delicate young lady." Prudence punctuated this speech with fluttering eyelashes.

Her sister was not amused. "I think you no longer have a conscience," she said.

"Constance, you wound me. It is not as though I have kept any of these things for myself," *though if Papa keeps going the way he is we may soon need to,* she added silently.

"I don't care if you are giving the money away. The point is, the jewels are not yours to sell! Oh, what does it matter if Lord Wentworth does offer for me? There would be no sense in accepting him, for I shall end up being hanged as a criminal," Constance wailed and flung herself from the bed and out of the room.

Prudence watched her go and bit her lip. She lay back against the pillows and stared unseeing at the wall. Maybe her sister was right. Maybe she shouldn't be doing this, no matter how worthy the cause or pure the motive. Suppose someone caught her. Suppose she had already done it once too often. Prudence loved her sister dearly and the thought of causing Constance to lose Lord Wentworth was unthinkable. But surely her sister was exaggerating. Constance had always been a bit timid.

Prudence continued to mull things over until her eyes closed. But even in sleep she didn't leave the problem behind. Her dreams were haunted by a series of accusing faces. Lord Wentworth pointed a finger at her and shouted, "You kept me from the woman I love!" Then his face faded, only to be replaced by Constance's tearstained countenance. "I tried to warn you," she sobbed and turned to watch the approach of a dark-clad figure. It was Lord Brimley, resplendent in full evening dress. "You used me for your own nefarious purposes," he growled, coming toward her with a measured tread. Nearer and nearer he came and when he got close she saw it was no longer Lord Brimley but the executioner, his face hidden by a black hood and carrying a big, bloody ax in his hand.

Prudence awoke just before her head was lopped off, but she rubbed her neck anyway to make sure everything was connected. "Oh, my," she sobbed, "what have I done?"

After that, sleep was a long time returning. She lay in bed, afraid to close her eyes for fear of reencountering that horrible hooded vision. Finally exhaustion won out and she fell into a dreamless sleep.

It seemed she had barely shut her eyes when Alice came in with her morning cocoa. Prudence moaned and, still in a stupor, threw a pillow at the invading abigail. Or was it the executioner?

"Mistress Prudence would never do a thing like that!" exclaimed Lilly when Alice returned downstairs with her tale of abuse.

"She did," sniffed Alice. "I've never been so insulted in my life. I've a mind to give notice this very morning."

Alice's sensibilities were soon soothed by a humble apology from Prudence and her affection bought by a gift of a fine shawl.

But an uncomfortable silence hung over the Pennhallow household that morning. Both sisters lacked their usual vitality, and they had little more than a mumbled good morning for their papa when he came down for breakfast shortly after noon.

Lord Pennhallow was not known to be a very observant man. And this was especially so at breakfast time as his interest centered on the food that lay on his sideboard. His lordship had a good-size girth and maintaining it naturally required much time and attention. But halfway through the meal he perceived an unnatural silence at his table. When he asked his daughters how they enjoyed the Sorenson ball there was none of the usual chatter about their doings. Constance managed a "Fine, Papa," and Prudence was silent altogether.

"What is the matter with my gels today?" boomed Pennhallow. "Are you both tired of town life already?"

"No, Papa," said Prudence, looking at her sister. "I didn't sleep well last night. I am a little tired."

"Yes, I am, too," said Constance.

"Well, you'd both better lie down this afternoon," their father huffed, rising from his chair. "Can't do to have you wilting before the season's over, eh?"

The only answer his enthusiastic speech received was a listless "Yes, Papa" from his younger daughter. Prudence appeared not to be listening at all and merely sighed.

Amazingly enough, the sisters revived instantly later that day, when Lord Brimley and his sister were announced. They were sitting in the drawing room, Prudence staring unseeingly at a book and Constance taking out her frustration on an unfortunate piece of cloth, her embroidery needle moving with more force than necessary. On hearing the name of her sister's latest dupe, Constance's eyes flew open and she jumped from her seat as though she would flee the room. Prudence gave a guilty start but recovered herself enough to present a tolerably calm appearance to their guests as Lord Brimley and his sister were ushered into the drawing room.

As they entered, Prudence couldn't help noticing what a handsome pair they were. Both were dark complected, with dark brown eyes. The sister was built on a more delicate scale than her brother, but had the same well-chiseled, classical features. Each had a frank and open face, despite their efforts to affect the currently fashionable air of boredom. In fact, both brother and sister wore a look that said, *I enjoy life and I am here to ensure that you do, too.*

Their friendly greetings assuaged some of the trepidation Prudence had felt all morning. "Good morning," she said. "This is a pleasant surprise."

Brimley smiled down at her. "I came to inquire about your gown. Will it recover?"

Prudence blushed guiltily. She forced a lightness into her voice that she was far from feeling. "There is every hope that my gown will recover to dance again," she replied. "But not this season, of course. Pray, won't you be seated?"

Brimley looked for the most substantial chair in the room and sat down gently. "It is good to see you again, Miss Pennhallow," he said to Constance.

Constance, though no longer terrified, was still nervous and could give him nothing better than a small smile as she sank back into her chair. She looked relieved when Angella engaged her in conversation, giving his lordship a chance for a tête-à-tête with Prudence.

"Tell me, Miss Pennhallow," said Brimley, "do you go to the Howells' next week?"

"Yes," replied Prudence.

"Then I hope you will save me a waltz."

"I shall be happy to," Prudence said and her suitor smiled his satisfaction. Obviously Brimley did not suspect her of anything more than clumsiness. She began to relax.

"And will we see you at the Havershams' rout tonight?" he asked.

"Most likely not. Aunt Louisa detests going anywhere that does not serve food. She will find some excuse to cry off." Prudence eyed her guest mischievously. "It will be a terrible crush, you know."

"I daresay it will," he agreed.

"And you still go? Yet you have no young sisters to escort, no one forcing you to attend something which no sane man would attend. You are most unusual, sir."

"Yes, I suppose I am," agreed Brimley. "But then," he continued, "I have been in town such a short time. I daresay the novelty of all these entertainments will soon wear off."

"Ah. A statement such as that leads me to believe you are mortal after all," said Prudence with a laugh.

"My sister can assure you of that," said Brimley. "Angel." He turned to his sister. "Miss Pennhallow thinks me a most unusual man."

"How so?" asked Angella.

"She thinks I attend all these social functions of my own free will."

Angella laughed. "Do not let the fact that he has no mama to force him to be sociable or single sisters that he is obliged to escort about town fool you. I am very much in need of his escort. Farnsworth hates these affairs and has as much as ordered my brother to give him a respite. So you see, he is not any different from the rest of his sex. In fact, it took all my powers of persuasion to get him to Almack's."

"What an unkind thing to say!" exclaimed Brimley as the ladies giggled.

"Yes. I am afraid it does rather tarnish your halo," said Prudence.

"Then allow me to repair my halo by taking you driving tomorrow morning, Miss Pennhallow."

"Prudence dear," said Constance quickly. "Did you not have an important errand to run *tomorrow?*" She looked at her sister meaningfully.

"I should be happy to take you on your errand," offered Brimley.

"No!" exclaimed both ladies in unison. "That won't be necessary," said Prudence in a calmer voice. "My errand can just as easily be run the next day. I should be delighted to go driving with you, my lord."

Brimley and his sister stayed only a few minutes more, the purpose of their visit having been accomplished. As soon as they were safely gone Prudence turned on her sister. "Whatever were you thinking of?" she demanded.

"I don't know. I was just worried about you getting rid of that awful ring. And you know we should pay a call on poor Lady Sorenson, whom you *robbed*"— Constance broke off her sentence to give her older sister a disciplinary glare—"and thank her for her hospitality, though I swear I don't relish it."

"I shall send her a note. And besides, we will see her later this week," Prudence said firmly. "Then you will see just how foolish you are being about all this. For if Lady Sorenson is going to discover her ring missing she will certainly have done so by the end of the week. And you may as well accompany me on my errand day after tomorrow. I am sure Mr. Biddle would like to see you again."

"I don't want to," said her sister stubbornly.

"Oh, Constance, please," Prudence pleaded. "Mr. Biddle is such a nice man. And I know he would like to show you some of the improvements he's been able to make because of our contributions."

"I don't want to go!" Constance declared.

"Don't want to go where?" asked Aunt Louisa, waddling into the room.

Both girls jumped. "Oh, Auntie!" Constance exclaimed. "What are you doing up?"

"What on earth do you mean, child? It is high time I was up. I understand Brimley was here," she said, turning to Prudence. "This is most encouraging, although you naughty girls should have had me with you to receive him. If I don't have two nieces engaged by the end of June I will be very much surprised. And I must say, the way your father's luck has been running I'll rest much easier when I've gotten you both settled comfortably."

Aunt Louisa wasn't the only one speculating on Cupid's activities. Lady Farnsworth turned to her brother as he guided his horses through the crowded London streets. "If you don't watch your step, Eddie, you will be posting your banns before the cat's had time to lick her ear."

"Such unladylike talk," said Brimley.

Angella gave him a sidelong glance. "I'm not saying I don't like the girl. But you must admit she is just a little . . . different."

"I am willing to admit that," Brimley acknowledged.

"Such odd behavior this morning," mused her ladyship. "One would think her bound on some nefarious errand the way they both screeched when you offered to accompany her."

"It is interesting, isn't it?" Brimley smiled. "I haven't had this much fun in years."

His sister sniffed. "Fun is one thing, but madness is quite another," said Angella.

"Nonsense," said Brimley cheerfully. "But I must admit I think you are right about one thing

—she is up to something. Do me a favor, will you?"

"Ask it," said his sister.

"Invite the Misses Pennhallow to tea."

"I see we are to pursue this acquaintance with a vengeance."

Brimley nodded. "You know I do not like doing things in a halfhearted way."

His sister shook her head. "Does that include falling in love?"

"How can one fall unless one throws one's whole self into it?" Brimley replied.

"Safely," answered his sister.

"I've been safe enough this past five years, Angel. And I can tell you I found it cursed flat."

"Well," said her ladyship, "I'll wager this little romantic adventure will prove anything but that."

Brimley patted his sister's hand. "Don't worry, love. I haven't fallen in love yet. I'm only standing on the edge, enjoying the view."

"Well, just watch your step," advised Angella.

Chapter Six

The Honorable Thomas Daltry did not pass his afternoon as pleasantly as Lord Brimley. He had an unexpected visit from a former friend turned creditor. A heated discussion ensued, ending with his visitor threatening to see Daltry in Newgate if he didn't settle by the end of the week.

Having begun badly, Daltry's day continued downhill. He ran into another friend in Bond Street to whom he owed money. Mr. Daltry's friend was sure he must have forgotten the matter of his vowel. It was such a paltry sum. Daltry assured him it had indeed slipped his mind, and he would call on him the next day to make good his debt.

Cursing his luck, Daltry scurried back to his lodgings in Ryder Street, his brain working all the way.

Something had to be done to reverse his fortunes—and quickly. He felt lucky and he was sure before the night was over he would be able to discharge the most pressing of his debts. But Daltry knew he needed something more permanent than a run of luck at the tables. Soon he would either have to take up his uncle's offer to buy him a commission or take a rich wife. Although both prospects were equally disagreeable, at least a rich wife would allow him to stay in London. So marriage it must be. By the time he reached his front door he had completely laid out his plan of attack against poverty: He would finish what he had begun and win the hand of the season's heiress, Miss Elyza Lansing.

He bellowed for his valet, a sinister-looking fellow whose shifty eyes and perpetual sneer made him appear more like a resident of Tothill fields than a gentleman's gentleman. "Lay out my burgundy coat," he commanded.

It was teatime when Mr. Daltry arrived at the Lansing town house on upper Berkeley Street and the drawing room was crowded with callers. But the look of delight on Miss Lansing's pretty face when she saw him confirmed that he had invested his time wisely. He bowed over her hand and graciously complimented her on her fetching tea gown. To her mother he said, "I am glad to see you looking in fine health today, ma'am."

"And I am glad to see you also enjoying good health," said Lady Lansing coldly. "And to what do we owe the honor of this visit?"

"I mentioned we would be at home, Mama," said Elyza, blushing.

Her ladyship gave her daughter a speaking look and recommended that Mr. Daltry try the cucumber sandwiches. She then turned from him and beamed on a pimply-faced youth who had stationed himself near her daughter. Her words to Thomas Bexton, the future Earl of Chudleigh, were as warm as her greeting to Daltry had been cold.

Mr. Daltry hid his frown and found a seat. The drawing room was stuffy and the cucumber sandwiches soggy, but Daltry stubbornly remained, waiting for an opportunity to get within range of his quarry.

Fortune finally smiled on him in the plump form of Miss Sorenson, who was able to pry Elyza away from her mama and off to a corner. Encouraged by a smile and a blush, Mr. Daltry wasted no time. Assured that her ladyship's attention was, for the moment, divided between her seed cakes and a pudgy admirer, Daltry discarded his teacup and quickly made his way to the two young ladies.

Miss Sorenson, seeing his approach, found an excuse to be gone, leaving her chair to Mr. Daltry. Elyza ventured a peep from under long lashes at the dashing man next to her and murmured, "I am so glad you were able to come."

"I am delighted to be here, even though I realize I am but a poor mortal grasping for the stars." Daltry's eloquence was wasted—Miss Lansing looked at him blankly. He tried again. "I realize, Miss Lansing, that your mother is not happy to see me here. And I fear you will suffer a scolding for having invited me. And since I should hate to be the cause of your suffering I think I had best leave."

This sounded so noble Miss Lansing could only beg her companion to remain. "Mama could not wish to exclude the son of an old friend."

"Miss Lansing, I am beneath your notice and your mama is well aware of it," said Daltry. "Yet . . ." He paused for effect. "Can a man be blamed for being unable to resist the temptation to look at such beauty?"

Miss Lansing bit her lip and blushed.

Daltry knew the heiress was fair away to being won. He also knew enough to quit while he was ahead. "I must leave now," he said. "Do you go to the Havershams'?"

Elyza nodded eagerly.

"I shall live for tonight." With that he took his leave, feeling well pleased with himself. Miss Lansing and her fortune were as good as his.

But he knew he would have to work fast. Her ladyship was a sharp woman. And as she had seen things warm up between Daltry and her daughter she had cooled toward him. She wasn't about to bestow her prize on someone who could really use it, he thought bitterly. His suit would doubtless never win Lord Lansing's approval either. If Daltry wanted the fair Miss Elyza he would have to convince her to elope, and soon, before her mother cut the connection. Of course he knew such behavior was totally unacceptable, but he suspected the silly chit had more hair than wit and with enough flattering speeches and longing looks she would be more than willing to risk a scandal.

Daltry smiled. The day had begun badly enough, but things were looking brighter. He was whistling as he left the Lansing town house.

Inside that imposing mansion, Miss Lansing was all smiles, too, and her soft brown eyes sparkled. She was even able to assume an air of interest as the pimply-faced future Earl of Chudleigh sang the praises of his newest purchase, a pair of sweet goers. Yes, she said, she might be persuaded to go driving with him and help him try their paces. Tomorrow? Well, no. She had an engagement. The next day? Miss Lansing was not precisely sure about the next day either, but one day soon she would be happy to go driving.

"Well?" hissed the fair-haired Miss Sorenson behind a plump hand as she and her mama were making their farewells.

"Bexton asked me to go driving, but I have fobbed him off," whispered Elyza. "There is only one suit I wish to encourage. He is so noble, so unselfish."

"And so handsome!" Miss Sorenson added in hushed tones.

"And so unsuitable," Lady Lansing would have added if she had been privy to the conversation. If that good lady had overheard her daughter she would surely have forbidden her to talk to the rogue who was trying to parlay a family friendship into a convenient marriage. Fortunately for her daughter, she had no idea that Mr. Daltry's friendship had already passed the nuisance stage and become dangerous. She knew her daughter to be a proper young lady and a most biddable one, who would do as she was told. It was in this comfortable belief that the Lansings presented themselves and their daughter at the Haversham rout later that evening.

Mr. Daltry was there, resplendent in his evening attire. His jacket was subtly padded, making his enlarged shoulders believable. His cravat was intricately tied and held in place by a diamond stickpin. His person was decorated by a fashionable collection of fobs and seals.

The object of his attention looked equally wonderful in her gown of straw-colored satin trimmed with blond lace. Her hair was in ringlets, bound up simply with a ribbon, and her hands were encased in white kid gloves.

In spite of the beautiful ensemble, however, the girl herself was, in Mr. Daltry's estimation, insipid. He found her to be little help in holding up a conversation of any length and was soon bored and glad of an excuse not to monopolize her time. "I dare not keep you talking with me long," he said in a low voice. "For surely the whole world will see my pretensions and suspect I wish for the moon." *And your parents will see and figure out what I am about,* he thought.

"Mr. Daltry," said Elyza, blushing at her own boldness, "surely you hold too low an opinion of yourself. After all, you come of a good family. And our mothers were friends."

"Ah, but that was years ago. And, alas, I am sure that even my late mother would tell me . . . But I should not talk so. And you should not allow it," he added with mock sternness.

Elyza's lip trembled and she looked up at him with big, liquid brown eyes. She opened her mouth as if to speak, but then closed it firmly.

She's close, thought Daltry. "I must leave," he said. "I am doubly fortunate to have seen you twice in one day." He bowed over Elyza's trembling hand and left.

So concentrated was he on making a dignified exit that he walked into Lord Brimley. He flushed and begged pardon while the young heiress continued to stare rapturously after him.

Foolish child, thought Brimley, watching Miss Lansing. His lip curled at the thought of his near collision with Daltry. The man was a fool if he thought he could win the Lansing chit with mere gallantries. Both her parents had more wit than to hand her over to a fortune hunter.

Brimley sighed. He was heartily bored and Daltry's foolishness had only served to momentarily distract him. This was a most insipid affair. The only woman worth talking to at the whole assembly was his sister and she was elsewhere, flirting shamelessly with several handsome young bloods.

In vain he searched the crowd for a pair of merry blue eyes and a mass of yellow curls. But Miss Pennhallow had been true to her word. She was absent. Brimley heartily wished that he was, too.

Chapter Seven

Prudence awaited Lord Brimley on the following morning with an air of anticipation. She considered herself above the sort of young miss who thought of nothing more than parties and husbands. But Brimley *was* very handsome and fun to talk to. Besides, ladies enjoyed sport as much as gentlemen, and reeling in an earl into her circle of admirers was very good sport indeed.

She smiled at her reflection in the drawing room mirror as she tied on her new bonnet, a confection generously decorated with ostrich plumes. "I do make a charming picture, don't I?" she asked, putting on her most angelic smile for her sister.

"I should hope so," said Constance. "Considering what you paid for that hat."

"Yes, but it was worth every guinea."

"No hat is worth forty guineas," Constance replied.

"You are the most unnatural creature!" exclaimed her sister. "We have already economized so much. And besides, if one expects to go on in society one must spend a little money."

Looking around the expensively decorated room with its thick Aubusson carpet and stylish furniture, one could clearly see that Prudence's papa felt the same way. Pennhallow had given his sister a free hand in decorating the house, which she had been happy to do until she began to suspect that her brother's purse was no longer as plump as it once was. Aunt Louisa had wisely curtailed her spending, so much of the house was not quite so *au courant* or splendid in its furnishings. But the Pennhallows had nothing to blush for in this socially important room.

"Well, well," declared Pennhallow, sauntering into the room. "That's a devilish fine hat you've got on, my girl. Something new?"

Prudence nodded, and her curling ostrich plumes waved giddily. "It was a little dear," she admitted.

"Nonsense. Nothing is too expensive if you really want it," said her papa.

Constance rolled her eyes and Prudence giggled. "There you have it," she said. "Papa has excellent taste and if he approves of my hat I know I have made a wise purchase."

If Constance questioned the wisdom of this reasoning as well as the purchase, she was prevented from saying so by the entrance of Ames, announcing Lord Brimley's arrival.

Prudence sallied forth to try the effect of her new bonnet on the earl. It was expensive, she knew, but all signs lately indicated that this might be the last season the family could afford, and she wanted to cut a dash even if she was to spend the rest of her life in obscurity.

The earl was properly appreciative. "That is a very attractive bonnet, Miss Pennhallow," he said as he handed her up into his yellow curricle.

"Thank you," she said demurely, "but I am afraid it clashes dreadfully with your carriage."

The earl cracked the whip over his grays. "I shall have my curricle repainted then."

Prudence dimpled. "I don't think it matches your tiger's livery very well, either."

"Alas, it doesn't. If I had only known. But let us hope that at such an unfashionable hour we won't meet anyone of consequence."

Prudence giggled. "Even though your curricle is an unfortunate color, it is a most dashing equipage," she said.

Brimley bowed.

"And your horses are . . . handsome."

The corners of Brimley's mouth twitched. "You are too kind."

"Yes, I am," Prudence admitted.

The earl shook his head and chuckled. "I was a

saphead to let myself get swindled so. Showy cattle but not good for much else." His lordship proceeded to tell Prudence how he had been taken in. Partway through his speech he realized this was no way to entertain a lady. There was something about this female that prompted him to do the oddest things. "I forget myself," he apologized. "I am not at Tattersall's. Let us talk of something else. But first, tell me how it is you happen to know so much about horseflesh."

"It is because I am not a boy."

Brimley raised an eyebrow.

"Well, what was poor Papa to do? No boys in the family. And I *am* the eldest."

"Of course," murmured Brimley.

"And although Papa is not a Melton man he is a very good horseman. Constance never had the interest—she has a very poor seat. I, on the other hand, am a tolerable rider and I've an eye for bloodlines. So Papa has shared some of his expertise with me. Have you met my father yet?"

Brimley nodded as the image of the stocky, rather loud little man he had met at Watier's came into his mind. "Lord Lucky" the baron's friends had dubbed him. He was allowed to be quite knowledgeable when it came to horseflesh. Yet he seemed unable to parlay that knowledge into pounds.

Brimley decided it was best not to continue this conversation and turned it into what he thought must be safer channels. "Tell me, Miss Pennhallow, besides being a most perceptive young woman and a good judge of horseflesh, what other talents do you possess?"

Prudence wrinkled her brow. "Goodness!" she exclaimed. "I can think of none. How very useless I am, to be sure!"

"You don't sing?"

"Oh yes. But off key."

"Then you must play the . . ."

"Pianoforte? It is said I can end the best of parties when I take my seat at that instrument."

He tried again. "Watercolors? Surely you . . ."

Prudence was shaking her head.

"Embroidery?"

"I detest it."

"What do you do to amuse yourself when you are in the country?" asked Brimley, suddenly at a loss.

"Why, there is much to do. I have my charity work in the village. And, of course, we have a well-stocked lib—I belong to the Minerva lending library," she said, quickly covering up her bluestocking tendencies. "And the local hunt is most exciting."

Prudence chattered away happily and Brimley listened, entranced. How lively the girl was. How innocent. How frank. There was no guile in her—anyone could see that. Surely his sister's suspicions were unfounded.

"We go on quite comfortably," Prudence concluded, unaware of how carefully she was being scrutinized. "Of course, Papa does give us occasional cause for concern."

She shook her head and sighed. "Poor cousin George. There will be no estate left for him by the time Papa dies."

Brimley knew he should turn the conversation

into more proper channels, but he decided to let the river flow where it would. He nodded sympathetically.

"Of course, the ideal solution would be to find Papa a wealthy wife. But for the life of me I cannot think of anyone who would have him."

"Perhaps a wealthy son-in-law might be easier to find," suggested Brimley.

"Perhaps," Prudence sighed. "Poor Papa. Mama knew just how to control him. And I think he only gets into mischief now because he has so much time on his hands. Without Mama he just doesn't know what to do with himself . . ." Prudence's speech faded to a whisper and she blushed as she realized the intimate turn the conversation had taken. "How very improper of me!"

"I shall not tell anyone you were discussing your papa's matrimonial prospects with me if you don't tell a living soul that I had no more address than to take a lady driving and talk horseflesh," said Brimley. "I am sadly out of touch with society. Pray, tell me how else do you amuse yourself?"

Prudence's face took on a dreamy look. "I like it best in the winter, when it snows. We build a roaring fire in the blue room and while away the hours reading. Or Papa and I play chess."

"Chess!" exclaimed Brimley. "I have never before met a lady who plays chess."

Prudence thought about this for a moment. "Nor have I! Is it not ladylike?"

Brimley laughed. "It may be a trifle bluestocking."

Prudence sighed. "Sometimes it vexes me greatly to be a lady."

Brimley raised both eyebrows at this. "But you make a delightful one!"

Prudence shook her head. "I should much rather be a man," she confided. "It seems to me men have so much more fun. And you certainly have more freedom."

"That is because we are not as valuable as the fair sex. Only a treasure needs to be so carefully guarded."

"How prettily said!"

"I am wounded, Miss Pennhallow. Confess that you thought me quite unable to make conversation with a lady. I am considered by many to be a man of intelligence. Come, tell me what you would do as a man that you cannot do now."

"I should become an expert swordsman," she declared.

Brimley dropped the reins and the horses took advantage of his lapse to enjoy a brief frisk.

"I have shocked you," said Prudence, hanging her head.

"No," he lied, trying to gather the reins and his wits. "You are, to be sure, a most original lady."

"Oh." She felt a resurgence of confidence. "I am only original at this hour of the morning. I am sure when you see me next I shall again be quite conventional."

"Let us hope not," said Brimley, and he turned the horses back.

As if sensing the need to prove how conventional they both could be, Prudence and Brimley maintained a conventional and rather boring conversation all the way home. Their parting was all that was proper and Brimley drove away with the hook firmly in his mouth.

Brimley was well aware that most young ladies were carefully instructed on how to behave with a gentleman. A very lovely mask was put on and not allowed to slip. His first wife had worn such a mask. It had stayed firmly in place until after their marriage. But Miss Pennhallow was different. Brimley knew she had nothing to hide. He smiled. What a handful that one would be!

Prudence, as well as Lord Brimley, was left with much to think about after their drive. She sat in her bedroom and nibbled a fingernail. What had possessed her to run on so? Did Lord Brimley think her an unaccomplished hoyden—or did he now suspect her of being a bluestocking? And what had made her blurt out her secret desire to learn to fence? She sighed in irritation. She had wanted to make a good impression. There was something about the man that seemed to bring out all the worst in her. She liked him, though. Such a ready wit. No witty sally, no matter how cleverly disguised, escaped his notice.

Prudence stared at the wainscoting, lost in a pleasant daydream. She suddenly shook her head. It's early days yet, she scolded herself. She pulled the ruby ring out of its hiding place. Besides, she thought, there is more to life than flirting with handsome earls.

Chapter Eight

Aunt Louisa was still asleep when the Pennhallow sisters set out the next morning on their important errand. So as to occasion no remark, the trip was concealed in a cluster of other important errands, including a search through the Pantheon bazaar for a yard of ribbon an elusive shade of pink and some Limerick gloves.

Since her nightmare, some of her sister's nervousness had begun to infect Prudence, and she found herself looking over her shoulder as they entered Hamlet's shop.

If Hamlet wondered at getting a visit again so soon from the mysterious veiled lady, he hid his wonderment well. His greed was another matter, and Prudence noticed the glint in his eye as he greeted her and her nervous accomplice.

He seated the ladies and Prudence produced her merchandise. Hamlet took the ring and examined it carefully. "This is most lovely," he said finally.

"Thank you," murmured Prudence. "Of course, I hate to part with it, but . . ." She left her sentence hanging dramatically and bowed her head.

"And naturally it is distressing to have to attach monetary value to something which most likely has great sentimental value to Madam, but

I can only give you . . ." He looked at the ring again. "Ah," he sighed, setting it on the table. "I am too softhearted." And he named a figure so low Prudence had to summon all her great acting ability to keep from laughing.

She took the ring and began to sob. "Alas," she said. "This will not do. I am undone." And with that she began to cry in earnest.

Hamlet began to squirm. "Since there is obviously such a great need," he said, "perhaps I can, just this once, go a little higher."

Prudence sniffed. A little more haggling and the job was done. The two young ladies emerged into the spring sunshine, one of them carrying a reticule much plumper than it had been when they entered.

The sisters waited to put their veils up until they considered themselves safely away from the shop. "That was a horrible experience," said Constance. "I am shaking all over."

"Never mind," said her sister. "Now you shall have an experience which will more than make up for it."

And Prudence was right. The sight of so many skinny, identically clothed children had the effect on Constance that Prudence had intended. Constance's eyes were teary as they left the orphanage, escorted to their carriage by the grateful Mr. Biddle, "How sad, how horrible!" she declared as they drove away. "Those poor children have no families, no one to care for them."

"But they do have someone," said Prudence. "They have us."

Constance nodded and dabbed at her eyes with a lace handkerchief.

The sisters arrived home in time for a sustaining nuncheon before setting out again with their aunt for an afternoon loo party.

"I don't know why I waste my time going to these silly affairs," Aunt Louisa complained as the landaulet began its stately progress down Grosvenor Street. "My luck is nearly as horrible as your father's. Of course, I know when to quit."

The girls looked at each other and burst out laughing.

"I must say," said Aunt Louisa, bridling, "things have come to a pretty pass when young girls fail to pay the proper respect due their elders."

"Oh, Auntie," gasped Constance. "It is too much, really. Why, you ransomed your favorite bracelet and that new shawl only last week because you were so sure your luck would turn any moment."

"Well, you will notice I am wearing nothing of great value today. And I brought only the smallest amount of money with me. However, if you see me getting carried away, one of you please acquire an instant headache and demand to go home!"

Prudence laughed. "It would serve you right if we didn't. But if your situation becomes desperate, dear aunt, you may count on us to rescue you."

The party was a small one and the majority of the guests were matrons. But some of the ladies had brought their daughters and the Pennhallow sisters met both Elyza Lansing and Miss Seraphina Sorenson there.

Miss Sorenson was already busy stuffing her plump form with tea cakes. She smiled, looking like a chipmunk, and beckoned to the sisters. "Isn't this fun?" she said, spurting crumbs. "Do you know, I won enough at the Lansings' last week to buy some Limerick gloves and a Chinese parasol?"

"I do hope I win today. Winning is such fun. Don't you agree?" said Miss Lansing.

Constance, who disliked gaming and was growing bored with the conversation, had begun to look around and was obviously not listening, so Prudence took over the job of spokeswoman and continued the conversation. She was still speaking herself when her aunt said, "Agnes, most likely you either lost the ring or gave it away to one of those mealymouthed hangers-on you're so fond of."

Constance turned white and grabbed her sister's arm, jiggling her teacup dangerously. "What is it?" Prudence hissed, following her sister's horrified gaze.

"I just saw the ring not more than a sennight ago," Lady Sorenson was insisting.

"Saw it?" snorted Aunt Louisa. "To be sure that is all you were able to do. You haven't had fingers small enough to wear it in years."

Lady Sorenson gave her friend a sour look.

"You don't suppose that new French hairdresser of yours could have taken it?" suggested another lady.

At this Constance tightened her grip on her sister's arm and Prudence gulped.

"Nonsense," their aunt scoffed. "If the girl was going to steal something she certainly wouldn't waste time on a mere trinket. Do quit boring on about nothing, Agnes, and let us play. I feel lucky today."

The other ladies, also anxious to begin, agreed. The subject was dropped and the ladies turned their attention to the serious business of cards. Both sisters let go their breath and looked at each other in relief.

But the relief was only temporary. As the play began Constance again caught her sister's arm. She leaned over and whispered, "What if she decides to search for the ring and finds it truly *is* missing?"

Prudence bit her lip and concentrated. "We shall have to hope that the Pennhallow luck does not visit us for a while. Perhaps we can each win enough money at loo to commission a paste imitation. I shall have to find a way to smuggle it back. Don't worry, dearest." She patted her sister's arm. "We shall come about. Just remember our orphans."

Constance gave her a weak smile and Prudence turned her attention to the game, determined to win a small fortune.

As it turned out the Pennhallow luck was dogging Aunt Louisa, so that her nieces escaped its notice and came away from the party considerably richer.

"But I don't think it is enough," said Prudence

later that night, eyeing the pile of pound notes on her bed.

Constance bit her lip. "Are you sure? It is only a small ring, after all."

Prudence chewed her finger. "I don't know. Good paste imitations are expensive. Well, we can try," she said.

"I have it!" exclaimed Constance. "We can ask Papa for some money. He won quite heavily at Crockford's only last night."

"Pity we did not know before," mused Prudence. "If he won last night he is sure to lose it all tonight, and more. Depend upon it. Papa will come home without a farthing. No. We had best see what we can get with this."

The next morning, while Aunt Louisa slept the peaceful sleep of the innocent, her nieces set out to do what they could to prevent fashionable London from discovering that a modern-day Robin Hood was in their midst. Once more they visited Cranbourne Alley. In spite of the veils Hamlet recognized his newest and steadiest customers.

"This is indeed a surprise to see you so soon, dear lady," he said.

"I have run into difficulties," Prudence confessed.

Hamlet looked alarmed. He hurried the ladies into his back room. "How may I serve you?" he asked warily.

"I fear I have been foolish to sell my jewels," said Prudence. "The ruby ring especially has such great sentimental value. And I am wondering if you could not make me a good imitation."

The jeweler looked relieved. "But of course. I can make you another ring so perfect none but another jeweler will guess it is an imitation."

Prudence pulled a wad of notes from her reticule. "Could you make it for this?" she asked.

Hamlet counted the money. He looked speculatively at Prudence. Then, as if having come to a sudden decision, he smiled. "For a trifling sum more I could have made something so perfect . . . but I understand Madam's circumstances. I shall do my best."

"Thank you," whispered Prudence. Then, all business, she asked briskly, "When will it be ready?"

"I think I can have it for you by next week," he promised.

"Oh, thank you!" exclaimed Prudence, rising. "It was very foolish of me not to have commissioned you to do this when I first brought in the ring."

"Most of my customers find it prudent to have a replica made of anything they wish to sell," he explained. "If Madam desires such a service in the future she has only to ask. Of course," he concluded gallantly, "let us hope Madam has no further need to part with her jewels."

"Yes," lied Prudence, "let us hope so."

Chapter Nine

"Do you think this plan of yours will work?" asked Constance as the sisters left Hamlet's shop.

Prudence nodded emphatically. "Yes, I am sure of it. Remember, we are invited to tea at Sorenson House next Wednesday. It should be a simple thing to somehow slip the ring into her ladyship's sitting room. Or maybe I will plant it in her daughter's room. That way she will think she gave it to Seraphina."

"But suppose after you get the ring there someone discovers it to be paste?"

"Oh, come, dearest. Most people are amazingly unobservant. How should anyone discover such a thing?"

"I don't know, but they might," insisted Constance, her voice rising.

"Shhh," hissed Prudence. "We don't want to attract attention to ourselves." She looked around. It was fairly early in the morning yet and most of fashionable London was still abed. Only a few men of business hurried past them and the streets were quiet except for the rumble of an occasional stray hack. Prudence was just about to lift her veil when she spied a familiar curricle coming up alongside them. "Oh, dear!" she gasped. "Try to look nonchalant. But don't turn your face toward the street on any account."

Constance, in a panic, did exactly that. Prudence grabbed her arm.

"It is Brimley," she hissed. "I recognize his curricle. Just keep walking. He cannot know us with these veils."

Brimley noticed the odd behavior of the two heavily veiled women walking ahead of him and wondered only for a moment what they were up to. But of course it was no business of his and he would have dismissed them from his mind altogether if he hadn't seen a landaulet parked farther up the street, and a familiar-looking footman loitering next to it. Brimley slowed his horses to a walk and stared hard. Where had he seen that man before? But the answer refused to come and as Brimley had other matters to occupy his mind he gave up the game. He gave the reins a flick and the horses broke into a trot.

The trembling women saw his curricle slow then pick up speed and move off down the street. "Oh, thank God," sighed Constance. "You don't think he recognized us, do you?"

"In these veils, how could he? And the landaulet has no crest on it."

"Do you think he would recognize James?"

Prudence shook her head. "Anyway, even if he did, he would most likely think we have gone there to get a clasp fixed or some such thing."

"Yes, but we would surely not do so wearing these heavy veils," objected Constance.

Prudence, for once, was bereft of words. Her brow puckered as she lifted her veil. She was more disturbed by the latest turn of events than she cared to admit. Not being able to think of an answer for this latest possibility annoyed her and she finally snapped, "This is absurd. Do, pray, quit teasing me about unimportant matters when I have so much on my mind!"

Constance was about to retort in kind, but they had reached the carriage so she held her tongue.

They rode home in silence. Prudence knew she had been undeservedly sharp with her sister. Normally quick to admit her mistakes and make up, she hesitated this time, fearing an apology would only reintroduce a subject that was becoming far too complicated. It seemed she no sooner got one problem solved than another one presented itself. How had she gotten herself into such a mess? And why had she ever thought this method of helping the orphans to be praiseworthy or fun?

Constance sat next to her wearing a face of stone. An occasional sniff punctuated volumes of unspoken reproaches.

By the time the carriage pulled to a stop Prudence could bear her sister's displeasure no longer. She leaned over and squeezed Constance's hand. "I am sorry I was such a crosspatch," she said. "Please don't worry, dearest."

Constance gave her a watery smile as the door was opened and the steps let down. "I suppose we must go to the Mayhews' with Auntie this afternoon," said Prudence, shifting into everyday banter, "but I would as lief stay home. I am fagged to death."

The season, however, was no time for rest and young ladies who insisted on going out before their morning chocolate deserved to be tired. At least that was what Aunt Louisa said.

But that night at Almack's Prudence got more sympathy. Brimley shook his head when he noticed her stifling a yawn. "The season's barely begun and its loveliest flower is already beginning to droop," he said. "This is not good."

"No," said Prudence with a laugh. "But this is how things are done. One can rest when the season is over."

"One could be dead before the season is over," he complained. "I see your aunt bearing down on us with your sister in tow. Do the Misses Pennhallow leave these hallowed halls early tonight?"

"It rather looks that way," said Prudence, watching as her aunt, clad in a very bright purple gown, came purposefully toward them, with Constance trailing reluctantly behind.

"Good evening, Lord Brimley," said Aunt Louisa. She nodded her head at Brimley and her purple turban bobbed dangerously. "You are looking well this evening, which is more than I can say for either of my girls. Of course, this is what happens to silly young females who have no more sense than to go gadding out on errands at odd hours of the morning, exhausting themselves so they are unable to stand up to something as simple as an evening at Almack's."

Aunt Louisa paused to draw breath and a furiously blushing Prudence hurried to say, "Auntie, we are not tired."

Aunt Louisa gave her an accusing stare. "I've seen you yawn three times from across the room. And this last quadrille, Constance was not paying attention and actually trod on poor Mr. Smythe's foot. My girls, we are going home this instant before one of you collapses from exhaustion."

"Auntie! Here is Lord Brimley waiting to claim me for the boulanger. It is too bad of you to whisk us off like this."

"Yes, well, Lord Brimley won't relish a graceless partner who yawns throughout their dance. In my day girls were made of sterner stuff. But there you have it. Anyway," she concluded, eyeing Brimley with approval, "I am sure his lordship will have no trouble replacing you. Come, girls." Aunt Louisa turned and headed for the vestibule, Constance following meekly behind.

Prudence turned to Brimley and dimpled at him. "She is adorable, isn't she?"

Brimley looked dubiously after the ample form of Lady Burton. Beauty was truly in the eyes of the beholder.

"Good night, my lord," said Prudence, holding out her hand to him. "I shall hope to see you soon."

It seemed to Brimley that he barely had time to reply before she turned and left him. She joined her aunt and sister and Brimley gazed after the Pennhallow sisters as they gathered their cloaks and waited for their carriage to be summoned. He would have continued to watch them until they had gone if an acquaintance had not stopped to talk to him and broken his reverie.

He stayed on a little while after the ladies left, dancing with Miss Sorenson and then with a timid young lady who was both delighted and terrified by the attentions of a handsome earl.

Then, bored, and having done his duty, he abandoned the pretense of enjoyment and went home.

The next morning Brimley decided to pay a call on his sister. As he walked up the steps to Farnsworth House, a liveried footman was descending. A light went off in Brimley's brain. He had seen that man somewhere. Then the image of two veiled ladies and a waiting carriage came to mind. Of course! He had seen that man just yesterday, near Cranbourne Alley. Who's footman was he? Obviously he served one of his sister's friends. Brimley smiled and shook his head. If it was one of Angel's friends, heaven only knew what they were up to.

Angella was still in bed when he presented himself and she sent a message for him to wait, leaving Remley to provide him with some of Foxy's best claret. "Rather a cold morning," he said, not turning from the fire as she fluttered into the drawing room.

"I imagine it is always cold this *early* in the morning," Angella replied pointedly.

Brimley turned and grinned at her. "And what were you doing last night that kept you up so late? I looked for you in vain at Almack's."

"If you must know," replied Angella, blushing, "Foxy wanted to spend a quiet evening alone with me last night."

Brimley gave Angella a wider grin. "What power you hold over that man," he said. "And what were you trying to wheedle out of the poor old fox now—a new barouche, perhaps, or merely an expensive ball gown?"

"Really, Eddie, you have become so cynical,"

said his sister, tossing her head and sitting down. "I suppose you are here to see if I have obeyed your instructions and invited the Pennhallow sisters to tea."

Brimley examined his nails. "Have you?" he asked.

"I sent John with a note yesterday. The ladies have accepted my invitation for Monday next. Their footman brought their reply just before you arrived."

"Footman!" he exclaimed. "Their *footman* was just here?"

Her ladyship nodded.

Brimley leaned against the mantelpiece, his brow furrowed. So the mysterious veiled ladies of Cranbourne Alley were the Pennhallow sisters. But what on earth were they up to? Why the disguises? Suddenly his blood turned cold as he remembered all the talk about what a loose screw Pennhallow himself was. What if the daughters followed in his footsteps? Something was certainly not as it should be, for proper young ladies didn't wander loose around Cranbourne Alley. What dark secret would prompt such odd behavior? Brimley began to search his mind for Prudence Pennhallow's hidden flaws. Was she addicted to gambling like her papa? Was she a fortune hunter?

Angella watched while Brimley engaged in this mental argument. "What is it, Eddie?" she demanded. "What troubles you?"

Brimley gave himself a mental shake. "Nothing," he said. "Something just came to mind."

Suddenly concerned, she asked, "Is there anything truly wrong, Eddie?"

"I don't know," he replied thoughtfully. "Entertain the Pennhallows, love. Then I wish your opinion of them."

"That will be easy enough. I must admit they intrigue me. The elder sister, especially."

"I am sure you will find her most unusual and entertaining—much like yourself."

"Should I thank you for that?"

Brimley smiled. "Wait until after next Monday. Perhaps you will," he said lightly, but his eyes were serious.

Brimley left his sister and headed for Jackson's to clear his head. Despite the warnings in his brain he was still drawn to this particular woman. If Pennhallow himself was a bit of a loose screw, it stood to reason his daughter would inherit some of his proclivities. Yet, other than some unconventional ideas, he had never before noticed anything sinister about Prudence Pennhallow. But why skulk around Cranbourne Alley in heavy veils unless . . . That's it, Hamlet's was on that street! Could it be possible that her father's extravagances had reduced the poor thing to pawning her jewels? The thought relieved him somewhat. Poor girl. What a fine pass that fat old toad had brought his family to.

Then Brimley's heart stopped. If he offered for Miss Pennhallow that fat old toad would be his father-in-law! Did he want to be the rich son-in-law he had prescribed to cure Miss Pennhallow's troubles? "Slow down, Brimley," he muttered. "Don't rush your fences." A fine lecture, he thought, but when had he ever listened to himself? And if he held back too long he might lose the lady to someone else. Brimley removed his curly-brimmed beaver and ran a hand through his wavy locks. Why the devil had he ever come to town, anyway?

Brimley's worries were instantly forgotten when he spied the Pennhallow sisters coming out of the apothecary's the next day. The lovely Prudence rewarded him with a look of surprised delight and the fat scoundrel who was his potential father-in-law was instantly forgotten. "This is a delightful surprise," he said. "I hope nothing serious brings you to the apothecary?"

"My abigail has the toothache and refuses to have the tooth drawn. I thought since I was out I would look to see if I could find something to ease the pain." Prudence shook her head. "She is such a pudding heart. I hate to force her to have it drawn. We shall try this," she said, patting the small package in her hand, "and if it does not work we will have to contrive some way of getting her to the tooth drawer."

"Mayhap this will work," said Constance hopefully.

Lord Brimley smiled encouragingly but ventured no prediction regarding the suffering abigail's fate. Instead, he mentally added another plus to his catalog of Miss Pennhallow's many good points—thoughtful of others. He offered to accompany the sisters on their round of errands and spent his afternoon happily carrying parcels, a job reserved strictly for servants and men in love.

When the shopping was done he insisted on taking the ladies to Gunter's to sample some of their famous ices, and by the time they left Gunter's Lord Brimley owed his good feelings to more than the sweets he'd eaten at that famous confectioner's. Prudence smiled up at him as they made their way down the street and he suddenly felt a ridiculous urge to skip. And while his lordship didn't do anything so undignified, his step definitely became jauntier.

He saw the ladies to their carriage and stood grinning long after they had disappeared down the street. This had been a most enjoyable afternoon. A pleasant vision of many more similar happy ones stretched out in front of him. Just think what he would have missed if he hadn't come to town!

Chapter Ten

At any other time of the year the sisters Pennhallow would have had time to study their troubles at leisure. But the London season was in full swing and Prudence and Constance were kept very busy with several drives in Hyde Park, two at-homes, a rout, a visit to the opera, and as steady a stream of visitors as any young lady of fashion could desire. In fact, they were so busy that Prudence was hard-pressed to find the time to slip away and collect the paste ring she had commissioned.

Desperate to visit Hamlet's, she did finally manage to get out the very day they were promised to the Sorensons. That afternoon, most pleased with the replacement ring, the sisters set out for the Sorensons' to complete their scheme. Constance nervously fingering her reticule and Prudence unconcernedly teasing Aunt Louisa about Lord Dudley.

Lady Lansing and her daughter had just alighted when the Pennhallows' carriage pulled up, so the guests went in together. As the older women greeted each other, Miss Seraphina Sorenson, all excitement and giggles, invited the other young ladies to her room to see her new ball gown, which turned out to be a white satin creation so full of ruffles and flounces it promised to swell Seraphina to twice her plump size.

As they were returning to the rest of the guests, it was a simple matter for Prudence to fake a fainting spell just as they passed Lady Sorenson's sitting room. With a delicate moan she collapsed against the door, the ring hidden in her hand.

The swoon was so realistic that for a moment even Constance was fooled. "Prudence," she gasped. "Oh, dear!"

Miss Sorenson and Miss Lansing stood gaping while Constance took her sister's hand and chaffed it. Finally Miss Sorenson recalled her duties as a hostess. "I shall fetch Shavely," she said. "He will know what to do."

But Prudence wanted no more observers at this

farce, especially a servant. Her eyes fluttered open. "What happened?" she asked.

"You fainted," her sister informed her. "I must say you gave us a terrible fright. Here. Can you stand up, dear?"

The other two girls rushed to help her up and between the three of them they got her to her feet. She swayed.

"Oh, my! Don't faint again!" squeaked Miss Sorenson. "Here, let us put her on Mama's sofa."

The girls dragged Prudence into her hostess's sitting room and helped her onto the sofa. Only Constance saw and understood the quick movement of her sister's hand under the sofa as she was gently laid down. She let out a sigh of relief and Miss Lansing, taking this for sisterly concern, patted her arm.

"I should get Mama," declared Miss Sorenson.

"Oh, pray don't," Prudence pleaded. "It is only one of my stupid dizzy spells. I daresay I shall be better in just a moment and I would hate to worry your mama for nothing. Besides, it is so embarrassing. Please don't tell her."

Miss Sorenson looked pityingly on her guest. "If you wish it, I won't," she promised.

"This must be awful for you. Do you have these often?" asked Miss Lansing.

"Only occasionally. Usually it happens when I overexert myself. I cannot imagine what caused this spell today," said Prudence innocently.

"Can something be done about this? Have you seen a doctor?" asked Miss Sorenson.

Prudence shook her head. "It is hereditary. My

mother had them as a girl. But she outgrew them. I daresay I will, too."

"We should return," said Constance anxiously. "Do you feel well enough?"

Prudence nodded and rose slowly from the sofa. Her sister caught her around the waist and Miss Lansing stepped to the other side of her while Miss Sorenson hurried to open the door for them. The four ladies made their way down the hall and downstairs to the drawing room with much whispered concern. Just before reaching the doorway Prudence motioned for her supporters to let her stand unassisted. Miss Lansing and Miss Sorenson, remembering themselves sworn to secrecy, immediately assumed such a convincing air of gaiety that each of their mamas turned a reproving glance on them as they entered.

As tea was poured Prudence couldn't resist bringing up the subject of her hostess's recent loss. "Did you ever find your ruby ring, Lady Sorenson?"

"Good gracious! I forgot to look!" exclaimed the lady, raising a plump hand to her breast. "I am glad you reminded me of it, my dear. I am going to have a complete search made of my sitting room and bedchamber. Though how it could have left my jewel box I don't know."

"Things do have a way of popping up in the oddest places," said Prudence innocently.

"Just so," her ladyship agreed. "That is forever happening to me. Why, only the other day, I felt sure I had lost my favorite green shawl, the Norwich silk, you know, only to find I had left it at

Elmira's, draped on the chair where I had been sitting."

"I'll have another of those cucumber sandwiches," Aunt Louisa said as she helped herself to the tray.

"Really, Prudence," she complained as they drove home later. "I wish you had not brought up that missing ring. Agnes was prosing on forever about it last week and we were nearly treated to another such monologue today."

"I was only being polite," said Prudence.

"Hah," her aunt snorted. "Surely you could have thought of some other way."

The sisters giggled.

"You may well laugh," said Aunt Louisa. "You have not known Agnes Sorenson as long as I have. Once she gets on a subject she will carry on about it forever. As if that ring would even fit her. She has gained so much weight in the last two years I'll wager half her rings don't fit. Just as well give 'em away and let them do somebody some good!"

"Maybe someday she'll do just that," said Prudence, smiling at her sister.

"I think it very unlikely. She will probably hoard them and pass them on to her daughter, who won't be able to get them on her fingers, either, although it is nice to keep things in the family. And it is nice to have a daughter to pass things on to. Not that I regret not having children of my own," she hurried on. "Burton and I had a good life together and he never once reproached me over our empty nursery. It wasn't necessary. His brother did his part to carry on the family name. And of course I always had you girls. Your mother was a good sort, always willing to share."

"We've been a shocking drain on your pocket," said Prudence.

"Nonsense," said Aunt Louisa gruffly. "Burton left me well provided for and I can stand it. So don't let's be talking about money now. And don't you girls be worrying, either. Your father's a good fellow, really. He'll come around. He just needs more to occupy his mind—sons-in-law and grandchildren."

Both girls blushed at this and Aunt Louisa chuckled. "You're good girls, both of you. The man who marries a Pennhallow will be lucky indeed. You've given your family nothing to blush for and I'm sure your father and I are both proud of you."

The sisters blushed again at this speech, as much from guilt as embarrassment.

"I thought I would sink!" declared Constance later that night, brushing cake crumbs from Prudence's bed.

Her sister nodded. "Yes. It was awful. And yet . . . I can't think that Auntie would totally disapprove if she knew."

"Then why don't you tell her," dared Constance.

"Maybe I will . . . someday. Are you going to eat that last piece of cake?"

Chapter Eleven

Aunt Louisa had insisted her nieces have new gowns for the Faversham ball, so the next day found the three ladies bound for Bruton Street, location of the fashionable modiste, Madame Fanchon. Prudence hated to see her aunt spend any more money on herself and her sister, but she couldn't help being secretly pleased at the prospect of new finery.

Upon entering the busy establishment the Pennhallow ladies met Lady Lansing. Naturally, greetings had to be exchanged and the upcoming ball discussed. The older ladies were soon engrossed in a discussion of their own, leaving the younger ladies to converse and idly watch the busy dressmakers bustle about carrying bolts of exquisite satins and silks in every shade of the rainbow.

Miss Lansing smiled shyly at Prudence and said, "I feel fortunate to have encountered you today." She hesitated, obviously wishing to say more.

"And we are glad to see you, too," replied Prudence encouragingly.

"I mean, I am even more glad than usual to see you," explained Miss Lansing. "You see, I have been hoping for an opportunity to speak with you." She lowered her voice. "I should very much value your advice on a matter of great importance. But we cannot talk here," she concluded, rolling her eyes in her mother's direction. "It is of a personal nature, you see."

"Could your mama spare you to us one day next week—Tuesday, perhaps?"

"Oh, yes, I am sure Mama would not mind that."

Indeed, her mother did not mind at all—how nice it was of the dear girls to take an interest in her little Elyza.

The Pennhallow sisters had indeed taken an interest in Elyza—a more than ordinary one. For now they were dying of curiosity. "What do you think she meant?" asked Constance. "You don't suppose she's fallen into some sort of awful scrape?"

Prudence considered this possibility and shook her head. "No. She didn't appear distressed." She shrugged. "Well, I daresay we shall find out soon enough."

The day of the ball Aunt Louisa guarded her charges carefully, not allowing them to leave the house. "You will not even venture near the door," she warned. "And you will both take naps this afternoon."

Prudence made a face, but her aunt remained firm. "We have been going too hard lately and I'll not take you to the Faversham ball looking as exhausted as you did last week. Nothing is worse for a girl than to have the shine taken off her before the season is half over."

So the Pennhallow sisters stayed home and napped, their faces and necks smeared with

Olympian Dew. Later they enjoyed a quiet dinner with their father and aunt, who together escorted them to the ball.

"I must say," said Pennhallow as they entered the carriage, "you gels look fine as fivepence. My compliments, Louisa. You've rigged 'em out in the first style of elegance."

"Yes, well, you can thank God I was around to take up the reins. I shudder to think what would have happened if the girls had to depend on you, Harold," said Aunt Louisa.

The sisters squirmed at this speech, but their papa did not appear put out by it. He held up a fat hand and chuckled. "Now, Louisa, there's no need to tell me what I already know. But dash it all, what do I know about bringing out girls? And you've no need to spend *your* blunt. I told you I'd stand the bluff for this and so I will."

Aunt Louisa closed the subject with a speaking look.

The Favershams' ballroom was lit with countless candles and the jewels of the guests glittered as they danced. But the brightest Indian sapphire had no more sparkle than the blue eyes of Miss Prudence Pennhallow as she tripped gaily into the room, a vision in her new gown, a high-waisted creation of gossamer blue over a silver underskirt. A shawl of silver netting slipped negligently off one shoulder.

Her court was already waiting for her and one of its members was quick in coming forward to claim his promised dance.

Constance was also claimed, by Lord Wentworth, who had been watching for her.

Aunt Louisa smiled at the success of her charges, and while Pennhallow went in search of the card room, she made a beeline for the punch bowl and Lord Dudley, who was doing his best to drain its contents.

Lord Brimley watched the entrance of Prudence Pennhallow with mixed emotions. For the man who wanted a beautiful and entertaining wife, the fair Prudence was a prize indeed. Not only was she a feast for the eyes, but she was also a lively and captivating companion. In short, everything Brimley had wanted in a wife. Yes, Prudence was desirable, yet something made Brimley hesitant to ask for her hand. Perhaps it was the vision of two veiled ladies skulking down Cranbourne Alley. Forgetting his manners, he spent the first part of the evening ignoring the debutantes who lacked partners and hovering along the edges of the dance floor, drinking champagne punch and watching Miss Pennhallow dance with her admirers. She was on easy terms with all of them and though each seemed most anxious to be in her company, Brimley didn't see that she preferred one to the other. The lady's heart was not yet engaged, he was sure of that. Yet Brimley wasn't sure it was engaged to him, either. He was no longer sure he wanted to marry anyone.

"I hope you realize you are making a cake of yourself," said a familiar voice.

Brimley smiled down into the teasing brown eyes of his sister. "What would I do without you to keep me in line?"

"I assume that is a rhetorical question since we

both know an answer would take much too long," said Angella. "Do show some charity and rescue Miss Wedgewood. She has sat out the last three dances and looks close to tears."

"Your obedient servant, madam," he said, bowing, and went off to rescue Miss Wedgewood from social disgrace.

Prudence, unaware that she was being closely watched, had been enjoying herself. With a copy of the ruby ring safely planted, she could breathe again and give herself up to the enjoyment of the dance. She also had the small thrill of anticipated adventure to occupy her thoughts. Of course, there was no sense in confiding in Constance. She would only worry. But Prudence planned to gain access to Lady Faversham's jewel box that night. After all, the orphans were desperate—her previous forays had only made a dent in the underprivileged children's plight. And now that she had hit upon the scheme of having everything copied, there could be no real harm in continuing her petty pilfering, could there? And, of course, the presence of the dashing Lord Brimley made the night complete.

She waited until the latter part of the evening to put her plan into action, first allowing herself the pleasure of sharing supper with Lord Brimley. She kept him highly amused with a witty monologue about the plight of a lobster whose love had been taken and put into the very lobster patties being served them and he was visibly sorry when the dancing resumed and Mr. Smythe came to claim her.

Brimley watched with a jealous eye as Mr.

Smythe led Prudence onto the floor for a set of country dances. He stood admiring her vigor until his hostess tapped him on the shoulder. She had a young lady in tow whom she was sure Lord Brimley had not yet had the pleasure of meeting. His lordship gave himself a mental shake and forced his attention to the business of being polite. Thus occupied, he failed to see Miss Pennhallow's dizzy spell.

The musicians scraped to a halt and the dancers left the floor laughing and breathless. Prudence was just complimenting Mr. Smythe on his improved dancing when she stopped and put out a hand. Her eyes closed and she swayed slightly.

"Miss Pennhallow!" exclaimed Mr. Smythe. "I say, are you feeling all right? Is it one of your dizzy spells again?"

Prudence nodded.

"Here. Take my arm and let me lead you to a chair."

"I think I'm going to faint," she gasped and faltered.

"Oh, no, don't do that! Look, here's Lady Faversham. Maybe she has someplace where you can lie down. And there's your sister." Mr. Smythe called to Constance and beckoned frantically.

Constance was with Lord Wentworth. At the sound of her name she squinted in their direction, then came hurrying over, Wentworth at her side. "What is it?" she asked. "Oh, dear. Prudence."

"Exactly," said Mr. Smythe, "Miss Pennhallow is not feeling quite the thing."

Her ladyship herself thoroughly enjoyed indifferent health and was always interested in a fellow sufferer. "Oh, poor child," she said. "It is quite close in here, even with the windows open. I was afraid this would happen. I myself have been feeling quite suffocated."

"Shall I get your aunt?" asked Wentworth.

"No!" the sisters exclaimed in unison. "I hate to trouble her over something so inconsequential as a momentary dizziness," continued Prudence. "I am feeling much better already, really."

"My dear young woman," Lady Faversham chided. "There is no such thing as an inconsequential momentary dizziness. Really, young ladies these days do not take proper care of themselves. Here," she said to Constance, "let us take your sister to my sitting room and have her lie down. I am sure if she can rest quietly she will feel more the thing. But we must inform your aunt straightaway. She would be most upset if I kept this from her." The sisters both looked so unhappy at this statement that their hostess relented. "I know what it is to be young. How I used to hate to miss a ball. Perhaps," she said to Prudence, "you will feel more the thing when you have had a chance to rest. But of course if you are not recovered in half an hour I shall have to fetch your aunt, my dear."

"Yes, ma'am," murmured Prudence.

Lady Faversham helped Constance settle her sister on her chaise longue and even went so far as to part with her vial of sal volatile. "I shall be back shortly to check on you," she said and left the sufferer to her sister's ministrations.

The door shut and Prudence sat up.

"What are you up to?" hissed Constance.

"You know very well what I am up to," she whispered and scrambled to her feet.

"No, pray do not," Constance pleaded as she followed her sister across the room. "This has become too dangerous."

Prudence opened the door a crack and checked the hall. "Good," she said, "No one is in sight, but we will have to work quickly."

She would have to work more quickly than she realized, for two of the people who had seen the small commotion she created downstairs were now on their way to her. One was Miss Lansing, who had been listening to some very pretty flatteries from Mr. Daltry, but no woman, no matter how charming her companion, could ignore the needs of a friend in distress. Poor Miss Pennhallow was suffering from one of her mysterious dizzy spells. Seeing that she was leaving accompanied only by her sister and Lady Faversham, and remembering how difficult it had been for three girls to convey her to a sofa, Miss Lansing felt it her duty to offer assistance. "I see Miss Pennhallow is unwell and I think I should offer my help."

Mr. Daltry followed her gaze and saw Miss Pennhallow being escorted from the room. "Such a large heart!" he declared. "But surely her sister and Lady Faversham have the situation well in hand."

"Oh, no," said Elyza, rising. "If she faints they will never be able to lift her."

Mr. Daltry smiled tolerantly at the heiress. "My dear, that is what servants are for. Look,

Lady Faversham has already summoned a footman."

"Oh, you don't understand," declared Elyza. "I must go and see that she is all right." And before her suitor could protest further she hurried after the retreating figures.

Aunt Louisa had also seen the commotion. She had been enjoying a comfortable gossip with Lady Sorenson, but she stopped in mid-sentence. "Now, what could be wrong with Prudence?"

"Oh, my, is she ill?" asked her companion, looking around blankly.

"If she is, I want to know about it," said Aunt Louisa and, excusing herself, she sailed across the ballroom, a puce battleship, causing all before her to scatter.

Upstairs, Prudence had just bent over the jewel box, her sister still remonstrating her, when a soft voice could be heard outside the door, calling her name. The sisters looked at each other in panic, then Prudence made a dive for the chaise longue. She missed, and fell on the floor with a thump, the wind knocked out of her. Miss Lansing looked in and saw Prudence sprawled on the carpet. "Oh, dear!" she exclaimed. "Has she fainted again?"

Constance grasped at this straw like a drowning woman. "Yes, that is it," she said eagerly. "She has fainted. She would get up, you know."

Miss Lansing looked in horror at the prone Miss Pennhallow. "I am sure we cannot lift her. I'll go get a footman."

"No, wait!" called Constance. But it was too

late. Miss Lansing had already swung the door wide and was fleeing for help.

Prudence quickly sat up and struggled to her feet, but the sound of two colliding bodies and a distinct "oomph" was enough to prostrate her again.

Aunt Louisa's ample form filled the doorway. "What is this? Oh, heavens, Prudence!" Before either sister could speak she opened her reticule and produced a small silver flask. "Never thought I'd need this," she muttered, pulling out the stopper and holding it beneath Prudence's nose.

Her niece coughed and spluttered and, arms flailing, sat upright. "Oh, what nasty stuff. Take it away, do!"

Louisa looked at the bottle in amazement. "My! I've never seen anyone come out of a faint with such vigor." Her eyes narrowed and she stared suspiciously at her niece, who now lay on the floor again, an arm over her eyes. "This is a most mysterious malady," she said. "You seemed well when we arrived."

Prudence rubbed her head. "I felt fine until the first dance after supper. Perhaps the lobster disagreed with me."

Aunt Louisa clicked her tongue against her teeth. "By your second season I should think you would have learned not to stuff yourself at a ball. Now there is nothing for it. We shall have to go home."

"Oh, but, Auntie . . ."

"I won't take a chance on your collapsing on the dance floor. You have created enough of a stir for one night and I'm quite out of patience with you. Really, a less aptly named girl I never knew." Aunt Louisa returned the flask to her reticule and struggled to her feet. "I am going to call for our carriage. I will send someone to help you downstairs. Please do not attempt to move in the meantime."

Aunt Louisa exited and the girls exchanged looks. Just as the accusations were about to fly Prudence noticed Miss Lansing hovering near the doorway. "Are you feeling better?" she ventured.

Prudence sat up and smiled. "Yes. Thank you for your concern." *And I hope it does not become a habit,* she thought.

The heiress bit her lip. It was obvious she wished to say something.

"Is something troubling you, Miss Lansing?" asked Constance.

"No. Well, yes. That is . . . oh, it is selfish to be troubling you with my petty concerns when . . ."

"Nonsense," interrupted Prudence. "You are our friend."

Miss Lansing fingered a ribbon on her gown. "Perhaps we should postpone my visit. You may not feel up to receiving visitors so soon after having suffered one of your dizzy spells. I know my mama would not allow me to do so."

"These spells are always gone as quickly as they have come," said Prudence. "I shall be completely recovered by then and sadly disappointed if you do not visit us."

Miss Lansing looked relieved—until Prudence got up with astonishing energy for one who had just been in a swoon.

"Oh, Miss Pennhallow, do you think you should get up?"

"Yes. I am much better now. And I certainly do not intend to be carried to my carriage."

Just then two footmen appeared at the door. All three ladies appeared perfectly healthy and the men looked at each other, puzzled.

"I am fine now," said Prudence, "and will not require any assistance after all. Constance, if you will give me your arm . . ." Prudence swept from the room, her sister in tow, leaving Miss Lansing and the servants to follow meekly behind.

The small parade to the front door was witnessed only by Brimley and Lord Wentworth, who had been hovering near the door awaiting news of Miss Pennhallow's condition. They broke into smiles at the sight of the Pennhallow ladies. And Lord Wentworth was quick to draw Constance aside to speak with her.

"I am sorry you are not feeling well," Brimley said to Prudence.

"Oh, it is all so silly. Such a fuss over nothing!" she exclaimed.

"A dizzy spell is hardly a small matter," chided Brimley.

"I suppose you are right," sighed Prudence. "I have never yet seen one of my sex who was able to keep such a thing from becoming a matter of national concern." She ruefully smiled and blushed. "And I have created just such an awful stir, haven't I? I do so detest delicate females, don't you?"

Brimley was about to assure Miss Pennhallow

that no one would accuse her of being one of that despised species, but before he could answer Aunt Louisa swept down on them and bustled both Prudence and her sister out the door.

Mr. Smythe came on the scene just in time to murmur wishes for a speedy recovery as the robust invalid was ushered out to her carriage. "I don't know why they have to go rushing off like that," complained Mr. Smythe. "She looked perfectly recovered to me."

Yes, thought Brimley suddenly. She did look perfectly recovered. His experience with swooning females was limited, but it did strike him as astonishing that a lady could recover as quickly as Miss Pennhallow had. Very peculiar, he thought suspiciously. Could Angel be right? Could the beautiful Miss Pennhallow really be up to something? But what? What mischief could a well-bred, closely chaperoned young lady possibly get into? Again, the vision of the two veiled ladies in Cranbourne Alley came uninvited to his brain. He scratched the back of his head in irritation.

Once again his wiser self advised caution. *Yes, yes,* his mind agreed. *I shall proceed slowly. I have not yet put my foot in a parson's mousetrap and I may still safely escape at any time.*

If his sister had been privy to his thoughts she would have laughed at him. Fortunately for his lordship's peace of mind, she was not, and he strolled back to the ballroom with a confident smile on his face.

Chapter Twelve

Prudence's ill-timed dizzy spell cost her dearly. While the other two Pennhallow ladies enjoyed Lady Wentworth's rout she remained at home, paying for her adventure with genuine illness brought on by the various home remedies poured into her by Aunt Louisa. Even something so mild as attending church at St. James was considered to be too much exertion for the invalid. So Prudence was left pouting at home while her family sailed off without her.

It took all her powers of persuasion to convince her aunt on Monday that she was well enough to take tea with Angella.

"I think she has been punishing you for embarrassing her with such a scene," said Constance with a giggle as the Pennhallow grays pulled their carriage off in the direction of Arlington Street.

Prudence made a face. "I suspected as much. Really, as if there isn't always some lady swooning at these big affairs!"

"Yes, but most of them don't make a habit of it," Constance pointed out.

"You may well laugh," said her sister. "You didn't have to swallow all those vile concoctions."

"I am truly sorry," replied Constance, swallowing a giggle. She lowered her voice. "It is the price you must pay when you rob from the rich and give to the poor."

Her only answer was a scowl.

The young ladies soon found themselves in front of Farnsworth House, a smart-looking brick pile. Their footman jumped down from the landaulet, went up to its door, and knocked. Remley informed him that her ladyship was at home and waiting to receive the Misses Pennhallow. That ritual over, the sisters were free to disembark and enter.

They followed Remley upstairs to the drawing room. On a blue velvet sofa, looking like a diamond on display, sat the beautiful Lady Farnsworth, dressed in a simple white muslin gown trimmed with blue embroidery. Her alert brown eyes greeted the Pennhallows with a curious look of anticipation. Her ladyship rose and glided forward to meet them. "I am so glad you could come," she said.

"This is such a lovely room!" exclaimed Constance, admiring the thick Aubusson carpet and the dainty knicknacks.

"Thank you," said their hostess, beaming. "I decorated it myself last year. It is quite my favorite room."

"I can see why," said Prudence. "There is something restful about the color blue."

Angella laughed and rang for tea. "I hope it does not rest you to the point of dozing off."

"No. I have had sufficient rest these last two days. There is no danger of that," Prudence assured her. Her hostess's look of polite inquiry made Prudence realize she had introduced a subject that would have been better off ignored.

"My sister is referring to her dizzy spell at the Faversham ball. Auntie made her stay in bed the last two days," explained Constance.

"That was horrible enough. But she insisted on dosing me with the most awful things." Prudence then proceeded to amuse their hostess with a description of some of Aunt Louisa's restorative home remedies. This led to some lively reminiscences of her past treatments for various family members and unfortunate dependents on the Pennhallow estates. "My uncle wouldn't allow her in his house for a month after taking the tonic she mixed for his gout," Prudence concluded and the three ladies giggled as though they were old friends.

But her ladyship had not forgotten she was charged with observing the Pennhallow sisters with a critical eye. So, not to be distracted, she returned to the subject of Prudence's health. "And are you recovered from your dizzy spell now? . . . Lemon?"

Prudence nodded and took the proffered cup. "Yes, I am fine."

"How uncomfortable it must have been. Let us hope it does not happen again. Of course, you have had these dizzy spells before, have you not?"

Constance at that moment overturned her teacup. Talk of dizzy spells was forgotten and by the time normal conversation was possible, reintroducing the subject of Prudence's mysterious dizzy spells was not. So Angella abandoned her spying efforts and gave herself up to enjoying her company.

And enjoy them she did. The three young women found they had much in common: a passion for pretty clothes, a love for the theater, and the conviction that the patronesses of Almack's were incredibly stuffy old dragons. Before the visit was over a new friendship had blossomed and the ladies were on first-name terms. They parted vowing to spend another comfortable afternoon together soon.

Brimley chanced upon his sister in Hyde Park later that day and was treated to an enthusiastic review of her afternoon. "We had a delightful time," she said. "I cannot remember when I have laughed so much."

"Yes, but I am sure you must have found something suspicious in Miss Pennhallow's behavior," her brother prodded. "Did she let some word slip that might betray some dark family secret?"

"Now you are roasting me, Eddie. And it really is too bad of you. After all, I invited them at your bidding. In fact, I began this friendship for your sake."

"And finished it for your own." Brimley laughed. "Never mind, Angel. I can see that you, too, have fallen under the Pennhallow spell and are just as trapped as I."

"I think perhaps you are right," his sister said with a smile. "And I think I should give you that dinner party now in honor of our entanglement. What say you?"

"I say that sounds like an excellent idea. Ah, I

see one of your cicisbei making his way toward us in a most determined manner."

Angella followed his glance and saw a foppish young man trotting toward her barouche. In addition to a supercilious smile, he wore a vast number of fobs and seals, which bounced to the rhythm of his horse's gait. His shirt points were excessively high and made him look like a turtle.

Brimley shook his head. "The warm weather does bring out the Tulips. I had better leave before I am quite cast in the shade."

"Don't leave me at the mercy of that simpleton," begged Angella.

"And when have you ever been at any man's mercy?" said her unsympathetic sibling with a chuckle. "No. My horses and I have both been still long enough. *Adieu*, enchantress. Maybe if you look bored enough you will attract a rescuer." Brimley tipped his hat to the approaching gentleman and trotted off.

Hyde Park was indeed crowded at five o'clock. With the exception of the Pennhallow sisters, who had been ordered to rest by Aunt Louisa, it seemed most everyone who was anyone was out enjoying the fine weather. Spring had come suddenly upon London and the day felt more like June than the middle of April. Ladies decked out in their finest adorned a variety of carriages, everything from park phaetons to tilburys. One of these carriages was shared by the Misses Lansing and Sorenson, accompanied by Lady Sorenson.

Mr. Daltry, who had been on the watch for his favorite heiress, was quick to make his way to them, but Lord Alvaney and Mr. Smythe arrived before him, and greeted him coolly. Miss Lansing's rapt gaze, however, was all he cared about. His competitors soon left and he took advantage of their departure by moving closer to her. "That is a most fetching bonnet, Miss Lansing. I wonder your mama allows you out in it."

"Pray, why should she not?" asked Miss Lansing innocently.

"Because you look so lovely that some buck may be overcome and, like Lochinvar, carry you away."

Miss Lansing blushed and Miss Sorenson tittered and her mama looked displeased.

"I have heard," he said, turning to Lady Sorenson, "of the good things the committee for the beautification of London is doing. Such a noble cause. Of course, I know you are too modest to admit it, ma'am, so I shall not press you to confirm the rumors that the great progress the committee has made is due largely to your efforts."

This speech had the desired effect. Her ladyship smiled and said he was very kind and, yes, the committee was accomplishing much.

"Do you ladies attend the Rolland musicale Wednesday night?" asked Mr. Daltry, looking at Elyza.

"Yes," she replied, blushing. "Will you be there?"

"I will certainly be there now," he said and tipped his hat. "I mustn't detain you anymore. Until Wednesday." He bowed gracefully, turned his horse, and left.

Elyza watched him go and sighed. "He is so handsome," she murmured.

"And so gallant," put in Seraphina.

"And so poor," added Lady Sorenson realistically. "Girls, you know as well as I the young man has gambled away his fortune. His manners are pretty, I will give him that. But remember, dears, it takes more than pretty manners to run the kind of establishment you are both used to."

The girls were silent. It did no good to argue with the older generation, for they knew nothing of love.

Miss Lansing sighed. "What am I to do?" she asked Seraphina later, as Lady Sorenson hailed a friend in a passing carriage.

"Don't be discouraged," her friend whispered. "Surely some idea will present itself."

And, as it turned out, one did—that very night.

Chapter Thirteen

Tuesday afternoon an obviously excited Miss Lansing entered the Pennhallows' drawing room. "Is your aunt here?" she asked nervously as the butler brought in the tea.

"No," replied Constance. "Auntie is taking tea at the Ashworths'."

"You may speak freely," added Prudence.

Miss Lansing blushed. "Oh, I did not mean that I did not wish to see her. I only m-meant . . ." She stammered to a halt.

Prudence handed the heiress a cup of tea and prompted their hesitant guest. "Miss Lansing . . . Elyza, can you not tell us what bothers you?"

Elyza took a deep breath. "I am in love!" she announced.

"How wonderful!" exclaimed Constance. "And does the gentleman return your affection?"

"I think he does," she answered modestly. "No," she corrected herself. "I know he does. Only, alas, he is afraid to speak."

"But I don't understand. Why should he be afraid to speak?" asked Constance.

"Because he has no fortune. I am sure he feels my papa and mama would never consent to the match."

"Oh, dear," sighed Prudence. "What will you do?"

"At first I wasn't sure. That was why I desired to talk to you. You are both so . . . assured. I felt you would know what to do. But that was before last night. It is the funniest thing, for the answer to my problem came to me while we were at dinner. Papa was talking about a splendid bargain he had made for . . . oh, I do not remember what it was for. I was not paying proper attention. You see, I was so lost in my own thoughts and worried about my own problems. But I heard Papa declare, 'That is the only way to get what you want, my dear—just go after it!' And when I heard him say that I knew what I should do."

"What is that?" asked Constance.

"Elope!"

"Elope!" the sisters echoed.

"Oh, no," said Constance. "You could not do such a thing. It would be scandalous. Your mama would be horrified."

"Yes, but once I was married there would be nothing Mama or Papa could do about it."

"Surely your suitor would not want to do anything to ruin your reputation."

"But it may be the only way."

"Oh, I am sure this man cannot be wholly unacceptable," said Prudence gently. "Who is he?"

"It is Mr. Daltry."

The sisters looked at each other. A glum silence fell.

"You don't know for certain that his suit would be unacceptable," Prudence finally said. "After all, weren't your mamas once friends?"

Elyza nodded.

"Then perhaps his suit isn't as hopeless as you think."

"But he has no title and no fortune," Elyza reminded her. "And I am an heiress," she added with loathing.

Prudence bit her thumbnail. Finally she said, "Has Mr. Daltry declared himself?"

"Not formally. But I know he loves me. Oh, Miss Pennhallow."

"Prudence."

"Prudence. If you could hear the sweet things he says you would have no doubt about his intentions." Elyza sighed, lost in a pleasant reverie.

Prudence sighed also, but her reverie was not pleasant. "What would you have us do?" she asked.

"Stand our friends should we need it."

Prudence nodded. "We will," she said, ignoring her sister's horrified stare.

"Oh, thank you," breathed Elyza. "I feel so much better for having asked your advice. Knowing one has friends who care somehow gives one hope."

"Rest assured," said Prudence, "we will do all we can to help you."

"How could you!" Constance scolded once Miss Lansing had left. "You should have told her that he was dangling after you only last season until he discovered you had no money."

"I could have. But do you think she would have believed me?"

"No," admitted Constance. She slumped back against her chair. "Oh, this is terrible. Daltry is a gazetted fortune hunter. I cannot understand why her mama doesn't snub him."

"She doesn't snub him for the sake of his mother. But you may be sure that even though she puts up with him, she would hardly welcome him as a son-in-law." Prudence shook her head. "What a dreadful coil. If I had not been so preoccupied lately I would have seen this coming." She sighed in exasperation. "All we can do now is watch them carefully and try to throw a spoke into their wheel." She sat up suddenly. "I have it! We could let it out that we have come into money."

Constance burst out laughing. "Oh, that is rich! Everyone knows we haven't a feather to fly with."

"Yes, but everyone knows Papa is a gambler.

What if we were to put it about that he won a sum of money and invested it on the 'change?"

Constance chewed her lip. "It could work . . . if we only told a few people, including Mr. Daltry."

"Yes," said a smiling Prudence. "A few coy looks and the mention of a sudden fortune . . . We could easily distract Mr. Daltry from Elyza."

"I don't know," said Constance. "It is all so preposterous."

"Yes, I suppose it is. Well, we may not need to use that plan. Something else may present itself. Anyway, the first thing we must do is observe him with Elyza and see how far things have gone."

"Yes, that is a good idea," agreed Constance.

"I'll watch them tomorrow night," Prudence said. "Then we will know better how to proceed."

Alas for the best-laid plans. Prudence was never to make it to the Rolland musicale.

It was really one of those unfortunate circumstances that prevented the Pennhallows attending. But later, when it came time to lay the blame somewhere, Aunt Louisa laid it at her brother's doorstep.

Aunt Louisa had persuaded her brother to escort them all to the Rollands'. Of course, Pennhallow hadn't labeled it persuasion. "Bullying, Louisa. There is no other word for it. I'm not in short coats anymore, don't ye know." Pennhallow shook his head. "Poor old Burton. Did you bully him like this?"

"You know I did not! There was no reason to

bully Burton. He was a sensible man who knew his responsibilities."

"Which I don't?" exploded Pennhallow. "Now listen here, Louisa. That is dashed unfair and you know it. Of course I know my responsibilities. Why did I bring you into my household?"

"Because you are a pinchfarthing," suggested his sister.

Pennhallow ignored this interruption. "Why do I have you here now? To take the girls around to all those dashed boring affairs that you women love so much. No one can say I haven't done my best for my gels."

"Now, Harold," said Aunt Louisa. "No one is accusing you of not taking an interest in your girls' welfare. But once in a while you need to come with us. Now, I have spared you from Almack's, not to mention three quarters of this season's most dismal affairs. It is a small thing to ask you to accompany us to the Rolland musicale. They are, after all, old friends."

"Humph," replied Pennhallow.

"Good. That settles it," said his sister. "And I'll hear no more complaining out of you, Harold, or I'll go back to Merton House and leave you to fend for yourself."

"All right, Louisa. There is no need for threats," said Pennhallow.

Of course, Lord Pennhallow was foolish and irresponsible, but his sister knew that once he gave his word he never went back on it. So when he was late returning home she didn't worry. She merely set dinner back.

However, as time marched on and Lord Pennhallow still refused to fall into step she finally had to admit defeat. The women dined without him and prepared to go on to the musicale alone.

They were just putting on their wraps when his lordship arrived. "Sorry, Louisa," he said. "I met Dalrimple at the club. Remember him? Hadn't seen him in years, you know. Time rather got away from me."

Louisa glared at him. "So I see."

"Now, Louisa, don't get your feathers ruffled. I can still escort you and the girls." His lordship hiccuped. " 'Scuse me. I'll just go and change and be ready in a trice."

He left the ladies waiting a mere twenty minutes, but it was long enough to irritate Aunt Louisa into a state of agitation. When he finally did reappear she jumped from her chair as if she'd sat on a pin. "Good! You are finally ready. Let us be going before we are unpardonably late. Really, I don't know why we waited for you. Prudence! Where are you going?"

Prudence was already halfway up the stairs. "I'll only be a moment," she called over her shoulder. "I just remembered I promised to return *Childe Harold* to Catherine tonight." She ran quickly up to her room and collected her friend's book, then dashed down the hall.

"Do hurry, Prudence," urged Aunt Louisa as her niece started down the stairs.

"I am hurrying as fast as I ca-a-a-. . ."

Chapter Fourteen

Prudence tumbled down the steps while the others watched in horror. Fortunately, as the staircase was rather short, she soon ran out of stairs and thumped to a stop on the landing, where she lay in a heap of pink silk. Her gown was torn and her carefully pinned curls had been oddly rearranged. One satin slipper had slipped off her foot and lay halfway up the stairs as if waiting for Prince Charming to collect it.

Her family had stood like statues while she made her bumpy descent, but when she stopped all three rushed to her, Constance kneeling on one side and her father on the other. Aunt Louisa had to content herself with hovering over them and wringing her plump hands.

"This is what comes of nipping at our heels and rushing us so," his lordship snapped at her. "Prudence, my girl, speak to me," he demanded, dragging his daughter's hand away from her forehead and chafing it.

"Where are you hurt, dearest?" asked Aunt Louisa.

"Everywhere," moaned Prudence.

"Oh, she's probably broken something!" cried Constance.

"No," said the sufferer. "I don't think anything is broken. But, of course, I can't be sure since I've never broken any bones and I don't know what it feels like. But my foot . . ." Prudence broke on a sob. "Oh, Papa, it hurts."

"Don't worry, my girl. We'll get you up to your bed and send for the doctor right away. Ames!" he bellowed.

This summons was unnecessary, for half the staff had heard the commotion and rushed out to the hallway.

"Yes, sir." Ames stepped forward.

"Fetch some brandy. Here, my girl," Pennhallow said, gathering up his daughter and staggering to a standing position. "Put your arms round my neck." Pennhallow grunted and staggered back a step.

Prudence cried out, fearing she was about to fall a second time, and Constance shrieked.

Lord Pennhallow took a run at the stairs. "Don't you worry, my dear," he gasped, "we'll have you all right and tight in no time."

"Oh, for pity's sake, Harold," said Aunt Louisa, "you will have her falling down the stairs again and yourself as well. Give her to James."

As James was a strapping young footman and in obviously better physical condition than his portly employer, Pennhallow reluctantly agreed. The transfer was made midway up the stairs with considerable grunting and shuffling about. Prudence closed her eyes and held her breath, fearing the worst. But fortunately the worst never came and she was able to again open her eyes and resume breathing as James bore her safely up to the second floor. He was followed by her father, who kept encouraging her to "bear up" and "be brave."

His lordship was followed by Aunt Louisa, then by a white-faced and tearful Constance. Finally, bringing up the rear, came Ames, bearing a tray with brandy and four glasses, having wisely judged that each Pennhallow would need a restorative by the time Miss Prudence had been put to bed.

The small parade made its way to Prudence's chamber where there was again much scurrying, everyone trying to be useful. Lord Pennhallow dismissed Ames and poured brandy for his daughter, then tossed down a glass himself. Aunt Louisa sent James for the doctor while Constance mindlessly plumped pillows, raising and lowering her sister's head each time she added a pillow.

"Do stop, Constance!" Prudence finally begged. "You are making me dizzy."

Chagrined, she did so immediately, letting Prudence's head fall yet again.

But the poor head was let fall only to be picked up by her father. "Here, my girl. Drink some of this," he ordered and poured a large amount of brandy down her throat, causing her to gasp.

"Harold! Now look what you've done," said his exasperated sister. "She's choking. Sit her up." She grabbed Prudence's bruised trunk and dragged her to a sitting position.

"I'm going to be ill," coughed Prudence. "Please, just let me lie down."

Both ministering angels let go at once and she fell against the pillows, gasping.

Her family stood staring at her for several moments while she lay with her eyes closed, trying to collect her nerves. Finally her aunt ventured, "Do you feel faint? Shall I fetch the sal volatile?"

"No!" cried Prudence, alarmed at the thought of yet another torture. "I am feeling better. Truly."

Lord Pennhallow poured himself another brandy, which Aunt Louisa absentmindedly grabbed from him and drank down.

Her relatives continued to watch Prudence in a most unnerving manner. Every few minutes they thought of something new to offer her. A pillow for her foot? Perhaps some laudanum. No, best not until after the doctor had seen her. Perhaps another drink of brandy?

On it went until the doctor appeared. A small, brusque man with gray mustachios, he examined his patient thoroughly and gently. "Nothing broken, but the young lady has suffered a bad sprain to the right ankle. She will have to stay off her feet for at least three weeks."

Aunt Louisa was horrified. "Three weeks!" she exclaimed. "Oh, that this should happen in the middle of the season."

"Unfortunate," he sympathized. "But the young lady will do herself considerable harm if she tries to use that wounded limb too soon. I would recommend she be kept in bed for an entire week. Then, if she wishes to, she may come downstairs and lay upon the sofa. I can see no harm in that. As long as she does not put any weight on the foot. Here is a draught to help her sleep." The doctor shut his bag. "It is a nasty sprain, but she appears to be a good, strong girl and I am sure she will have a speedy recovery and no harm done." The doctor smiled encouragingly at Prudence.

If Aunt Louisa thought of missing three weeks of London's social season as no harm done she kept those thoughts to herself.

As for Prudence, she received the news of her imprisonment stoically. Only one tear escaped her eyes as she listened to the doctor's instructions.

"It won't be so bad," Constance consoled her after he left. "The doctor did not say you couldn't have visitors and next week we shall move you down to the drawing room and entertain lavishly. And I shall not go out until you are well and able to go out with me."

"You certainly will do no such thing!" declared her aunt. "It is horrible enough that your sister must be out for a full three weeks. I cannot afford you to be out of circulation, too. If we accomplish nothing else this year, we will at least bring Lord Wentworth up to scratch."

Constance, usually a very biddable girl, turned mulish and refused to be gay and dissipated while her own dear sister lay on a bed of pain.

Even Prudence saw the foolishness of this resolve. "Auntie is right," she said. "We must be practical. Don't worry about me. Just keep me supplied with something good to read and I shall be fine."

Prudence soon had herself and her sister convinced that she would, indeed, be fine. But that was before an invitation arrived the next day from Lady Farnsworth, bidding the Pennhallow sisters to a small dinner party. "Nothing formal, you understand," the note read. "But plenty of good company and good conversation." Prudence's lower lip trembled as she read the note.

Constance saw a slow tear slip down her sister's cheek. "Perhaps when she hears, Angella will postpone her dinner party."

"That would hardly be fair to her other guests." Prudence sighed. "I should so like to have gone."

"I will write Angella and explain why we cannot accept," said Constance, rising.

"There is no reason why you cannot go," urged Prudence.

"No. This invitation was as much for your sake as for mine—possibly more. I shall write to Angella immediately and explain what has happened." And with that Constance left the invalid.

Aunt Louisa came to Prudence's room a little later to check on her niece and found her despondent. "Blue-deviled, my girl?"

"Auntie!" Prudence managed to smile. "You startled me."

"Come now, tell your old aunt what has upset you."

" 'Tis nothing much. I was just feeling a little sorry for myself, I suppose."

"It wouldn't have anything to do with missing Lady Farnsworth's dinner party, would it?" Aunt Louisa looked fondly at her surprised niece. "Yes, love. I know. Your sister just told me." She smiled at Constance, who had just entered the room and was looking at her sister with concern. "This is a stroke of terrible luck," said Aunt Louisa, patting

Prudence's hand. "But even the worst luck can
turn when we least expect it."

Prudence shrugged. The lump in her throat
made it impossible for her to speak.

"Oh, Auntie!" exclaimed Constance. "We just
cannot gad about every evening and leave poor
Prudence here all by herself. It is too, too cruel."

"Yes," her aunt sighed. "I must say I agree with
you."

So the ladies consulted their social calendar.
"We must go to the Wentworths' dinner party
next week," said Aunt Louisa. "And the Debenham ball is also coming up."

"Here," said Constance. "We are engaged to
the Sorensons for dinner next week also. Can we
not cancel that?"

Aunt Louisa shook her head. "No. We had best
not. But it looks as if that is really the only other
pressing engagement we have. All others we may
cancel. And I think Almack's will survive our ab-
sence. Although, on second thought, we had better go at least once—it wouldn't be wise to drop
out of sight completely."

"Besides," added Prudence later, when the sisters were alone, "someone has got to observe our
poor Elyza and Mr. Daltry. I obviously cannot do
it now, so it is up to you, dearest, to keep an eye
on her. And if things come to a head before I am
up and about, you may have to draw him away
from her."

Constance turned pale. "I?"

"Come now," said Prudence briskly. "You
don't wish to see Elyza seduced by a cold-hearted
fortune hunter, do you?"

Constance shook her head.

"Then you must be willing to do this." Prudence patted her sister's hand. "There is no need to get into a taking yet. Things may not be as bad as we think. But do keep your wits about you and keep a watchful eye on Elyza."

So it was settled. Prudence resigned herself to invalidism—something that was much easier to do after receiving a note from Angella wishing her a speedy recovery and promising to postpone her party until both sisters could attend. "With Constance to enliven my days I will be the merriest invalid in London," she declared.

After four days, however, the merriest invalid in London had turned into the grumpiest. "I know every flower on the wainscoting," she complained on the fifth day of her incarceration.

Constance patted her hand. "I know it is hard, but the doctor said—"

"I know what the doctor said. But it is my foot, and my foot, like the rest of me, is tired of this bed. I must get up or I shall go mad. So please bring James and Edgar here in half an hour. I shall be able to get downstairs perfectly well if I can lean on them."

"I am not sure Auntie will like this," said Constance.

"I know she will not. That is why I want to get downstairs before she is up."

Half an hour later, the footmen presented themselves and found their mistress standing in the doorway and ready to make her pilgrimage to the drawing room.

By the time Aunt Louisa was up, her headstrong niece was comfortably established and feeling none the worse for her escape. "You wicked girl!" exclaimed Aunt Louisa. "You heard the doctor—one week in bed."

"Oh, Auntie, it has been nearly a week. And besides, with the aid of James and Edgar, my right foot never so much as touched the ground, I promise you. Please let me stay. It was so dreadful being confined to my room. I felt quite cut off."

"I do not see how you could possibly feel cut off when your sister is practically living in there with you," protested Aunt Louisa.

"I don't know how, either," Prudence admitted. "But I did."

This discussion might have continued for the better part of the afternoon had not Ames appeared with Angella's card. On it was scribbled a polite request to see the invalid.

"Oh, company at last!" exclaimed Prudence. "Show her in, please."

Aunt Louisa tried to look stern and failed. "All right, miss," she said. "Circumstances seem to have a way of rewarding your little rebellions. But take care, for circumstances may not always be your friend."

Chapter Fifteen

The "her" turned out to be a "them," for Ames returned with not only Angella but also her brother. At the sight of him, Prudence's hands flew to her hair and she found herself, for some odd reason, blushing.

"We thought you might not be up to receiving callers but wanted to be among the first to wish you a speedy recovery," said Angella.

"If three weeks is your idea of a speedy recovery, you may wish it," said Prudence, smiling.

"Three weeks!" Her ladyship was horrified.

"But at least I am allowed to have visitors," said Prudence. "Do sit down. You have saved me from a fate worse than death and I am truly grateful."

"And what is that?" asked Brimley. He sat down on one of the delicate chairs Prudence had indicated. It creaked ominously under his weight and he grimaced.

His sister giggled. "Do tell us. From what horrible fate have we delivered you?"

"Auntie was about to make me return to my bedchamber and I have already been there four days."

"The doctor said a week," Aunt Louisa defended herself. "And I certainly hope you do not suffer a setback."

"It has been my observation," said Brimley, "that doctors are a rather cautious lot. Miss Pennhallow does not appear to have suffered any from her escape."

Aunt Louisa was not about to be mollified. She shook her head as she rang for Ames. "Next thing she'll be wanting to jaunt off to a ball. Tea, please, Ames."

"No, dear Aunt," said Prudence. "I will not tease you to that extent, I promise. Although I must admit this inactivity chaffs me horribly."

"We shall have to do all in our power to make your convalescence a pleasant one," said her ladyship.

"Thank you, Angella. And thank you so much for postponing your dinner party. Although I wish you hadn't done it on my account."

"Nonsense," replied Angella. "I promised my brother this dinner party when he first came to town, but Eddie is on no schedule and I am sure he would as lief wait until we can include you, for you must know you were both at the top of our guest list."

Prudence blushed, feeling Lord Brimley's gaze upon her and again murmured her thanks.

"I hope your fall was not caused by one of your dizzy spells," Angella said to Prudence.

Prudence blushed guiltily as Aunt Louisa, having heard a part of this remark, said, "Dizzy spells? What's this about dizzy spells?"

"Angella was asking how I happened to fall down the stairs," Prudence replied. "It was very clumsy of me, but I was in a hurry and caught my foot on the carpet," she explained, careful to omit that her toe had caught in a tear in the worn carpet.

Refreshments were brought in and the conversation continued to flow. In fact, it flowed so continuously that the visitors were amazed to discover when Brimley finally looked at his watch that they had stayed much longer than they intended.

"How impolite of us," said his sister. "Dear Lady Burton, please forgive us. We should not have stayed so long on your niece's first day out of the sickroom."

"Nonsense," said Aunt Louisa. " 'Tis not her voice that is sprained. In fact," she added in a whisper, "I think it has done her good. For a girl of Prudence's temperament isolation is a terrible thing."

Meanwhile Brimley was making Prudence an interesting offer. "If your sister or aunt would play chaperon I have something which I think might amuse you. I should like to bring it tomorrow afternoon if I may."

"I am most intrigued," said Prudence. She looked at her sister. "Constance?"

"I would be happy to help," she answered.

"Thank you." Brimley bowed. "Until tomorrow, then?"

After the visitors left, Aunt Louisa poured herself another cup of tea and looked at her niece approvingly. "Well, you sly puss. Things may turn out after all. Who would have thought spraining an ankle in the middle of the season would turn out to be such a stroke of luck. I think maybe we should give it out to your other admirers that you are not yet up to having vistors. A few uninterrupted tête-à-têtes with his lordship may be all that is needed to do the trick."

"Oh, Auntie." Prudence blushed.

The next day Lord Brimley was ushered into the Pennhallow drawing room carrying a tooled leather box.

The sisters watched with interest as he opened it and drew out a chessboard, which he laid out on the game table. "How delightful!" Prudence exclaimed.

"Since you first mentioned your interest in the game, I have wanted to pit myself against you, Miss Pennhallow," he said as he arranged the carved ivory pieces on the board.

Prudence's hand was already hovering over the chessboard, but she drew it back. "Perhaps we should not play," she said, giving Brimley an arch look.

"Why not?" he demanded.

"Because I am not one of those deceptive females who would deliberately lose to flatter a man's vanity. In fact, I would try my hardest to beat you. And if I were to win the game, maybe I would lose a friend."

"Since I never lose, I think, Miss Pennhallow, that my good opinion of myself will remain intact."

Prudence smiled. "Somehow I knew you would say that. Let us begin," she said, picking up a pawn and moving it forward decisively.

The game lasted two hours. Prudence and Brimley sat in intense concentration and after an hour the only sound in the room was the ticking of the clock and the gentle snoring of their young chaperon, who had tired of keeping up with the complex moves. "You are in check, my lord," Prudence declared at last.

"Ah, but I am not without hope," replied his lordship calmly.

Twenty minutes later he moved his rook opposite her king and murmured, "Checkmate."

Prudence sighed and leaned back against the sofa.

Brimley looked at her from under his eyebrows.

"When we began this game you had my promise I would remain your friend if you won, but you gave me no such assurance in return," said Brimley. "Friends?"

"Of course! On one condition."

"What is that?"

"You must promise to give me a chance for revenge."

His lordship grinned. "Shall I come tomorrow?"

"Would you?" asked Prudence. "Although I must confess that after having seen what a formidable opponent you are, I have little hope of winning."

"Nonsense. You played a very good game. I think I may know some moves which you do not and that gives me a definite advantage."

"You are a truly chivalrous winner," she said, "and such kindness shames me, for had it been I who won I should have gloated horribly."

"Will your sister mind spending another such

afternoon?" Brimley nodded in the direction of the sleeping beauty.

"No. But she will most likely have some needlework with her tomorrow. I daresay she will be embarrassed at having fallen asleep while on duty."

"Let us not wake her then," he suggested. "Shall I leave the set here in your care until tomorrow?"

"If you wish."

"Very good." Brimley rose and stretched his long legs. "Thank you for a most pleasant afternoon, Miss Pennhallow," he said, bowing over her hand.

"It is I who should thank you for giving up an afternoon to entertain an invalid. I certainly am not fond of losing, but this is the first day since my fall that I have enjoyed being laid up."

And so began a camaraderie between Miss Prudence Pennhallow and Lord Brimley. They enjoyed a week of chess and banter, uninterrupted by anyone save Constance and occasionally Aunt Louisa, who delighted in entering the room on the flimsiest of excuses so she could observe the progress of her niece's budding romance.

The more time he spent with Miss Pennhallow, the more Brimley found himself drawn to her. And the more necessary it became to ignore those niggling doubts at the back of his mind. Her frankness of manner convinced him that whatever strange business her family was about couldn't be as bad as he had at first suspected. There was too much good in Miss Prudence

Pennhallow to allow her to become involved in anything very havey-cavey.

Miss Pennhallow herself was also enjoying his lordship's visits. What was it that made her heart race when he first entered the drawing room— could it be love? Surely it must be something like it, for no other gentleman of her acquaintance affected her this way.

The idyll ended the afternoon Mr. Smythe finally managed to get past the guards. Aunt Louisa was gone and had neglected to tell Ames that, as usual, Miss Prudence was not up to receiving visitors. So Mr. Smythe was duly announced and ushered in.

Mr. Smythe was shocked to discover Miss Pennhallow involved in anything as intellectual as a game of chess. "Oh, uh, I say. Am I interrupting something?" he stammered.

"Positively," said Brimley.

"But come sit down anyway," offered Prudence.

Mr. Smythe seated himself on the sofa, close to the two gamesters. "Never mastered the game myself."

"But you have other talents, I am sure," murmured Brimley.

Prudence covered a smile. "How are you, Mr. Smythe?"

"I am fine. I came to see how you are doing. You know your aunt has been keeping visitors at bay." Mr. Smythe looked at Brimley. "Most of 'em anyway, with a tale of you not being up to callers."

"As you see I am now well enough," said Prudence. "Alas, I still have nearly another two weeks before I may go out."

"No!" exclaimed Mr. Smythe. "I call that cursed unfair. Surely it won't take you that long to mend. Things are sadly flat without you, you know."

"I should hope so," she said with a laugh. "But I am afraid I must remain a prisoner for another two weeks. The doctor insisted."

"Well, if you can't come to your friends, they will just have to come to you. We will do all that is in our power to keep your spirits up."

Mr. Smythe was as good as his word. He returned the next day with Lord Alvaney and the day after that brought Miss Sorenson and Miss Lansing. The quiet afternoons with Lord Brimley were at an end. "You may as well pack up the chess set," she told him sadly one afternoon as her drawing room buzzed with visitors. "For we shall never have a chance to play now. And I was sure I would beat you. How I would have loved to finish that game," she added wistfully.

"Maybe someday we will," said Brimley.

There was no mistaking the earl's expression. Prudence felt the blood rush up her neck and spread to her cheeks. She lowered her eyes and said softly, "I would enjoy that, I'm sure."

Brimley allowed himself a moment to look at her tenderly, then lightened his voice and conversation.

The moment passed, but the warm feelings lingered after the guests had departed. Prudence was distracted the rest of the day. That evening, she gave her aunt and sister such a cheery farewell when they left for the Debenham ball that Aunt Louisa couldn't help wondering aloud what she was up to that made her so anxious to be rid of them.

"Auntie! I am deeply hurt. Pray, what mischief could I possibly get into?"

"I don't know. That is what worries me."

Prudence laughed and blew them a kiss. Then she settled back on the pillows, opened her book, and dreamed of Lord Brimley. She took her pleasant daydreams with her into sleep and awakened the next morning in perfect charity with the entire world.

Constance, however, looked quite the opposite. She entered her sister's bedroom while Prudence was still enjoying her morning chocolate, perched on the bed, and glared at her.

"You did not sleep well," said Prudence.

"You are right. And it is all your fault."

"My fault? How can that be? I have done nothing."

"That is right. You have done nothing. It is I who has had to bear the full responsibility for Elyza's future."

Prudence jerked up, spilling her cocoa. "Is it that bad?"

Constance nodded. "I watched them at the ball last night. Or at least I tried, but it is very difficult to watch someone from a discreet distance and be nonchalant about it. I was forever having to make up foolish excuses to be near them when they stood together. I am sure Lord Wentworth thinks I am a perfect cake."

"Oh, come now, dearest. We both know he thinks no such thing," said Prudence. "What makes you think things are so desperate?"

"Because I happened to follow them into the conservatory. It was most embarrassing, really."

"Yes, dear, but what did you *see?*" prompted Prudence.

"I saw him kiss her hand."

"Oh!" exclaimed Prudence, exasperated.

"In a *most* familiar manner," her sister continued. "And I am not sure, but I think I heard him call her dearest, though I cannot be sure of that because he was speaking softly and my dress rustled so he heard me and broke off what he was saying. In fact, they both stepped apart, looking quite guilty. Oh, I was so embarrassed! Although I did mumble something about meeting someone and left immediately. But I am sure Elyza knows I was spying on her. And I was and I *do* hate it!"

"Yes, but it is for her own good. Remember that."

Constance sighed. "What are we to do?"

"Let me think a moment," said Prudence. She sat studying her empty cup. "I know! Go see Elyza today and tell her we wish to help her."

"What?"

"Tell her we wish to help her. And you must convince her that she cannot carry off an elopement without our help. But tell her she must wait until my ankle is healed and I can go out."

"Then what?"

"I do not know," Prudence confessed. "But at least this will give us time to think of some way to save her."

"I do hope some way of drawing him off presents itself to us soon," said Constance.

Chapter Sixteen

The day finally came when the doctor pronounced Miss Pennhallow able to reenter the social whirl. "But do take care. Not too much standing or dancing your first night out."

Prudence promised to practice moderation and her aunt allowed her to venture out for a carriage ride with Constance in Hyde Park, where she encountered Lord Brimley.

"Miss Pennhallow, it is wonderful to see you up and about again," he said, pulling up his horse alongside the landaulet. "In fact, this is a double delight, seeing both the Pennhallow sisters," he added. Constance rewarded him with a very pretty smile. He turned again to Prudence. "Does this mean you are recovered enough to attend the Everlys' ball next week?"

"It certainly does," said Prudence. "And I am so looking forward to it."

"The life of an invalid no longer suits you?" he asked.

"Goodness, how would she know?" exclaimed Constance, laughing.

Prudence smiled shyly. "Yes, I was a very merry invalid, was I not? Thanks to all my kind friends."

"Keeping you entertained was truly our pleasure, Miss Pennhallow," Brimley said meaningfully. Blue eyes met brown and Prudence blushed prettily. Her color deepened as his lordship smiled fondly at her. "May I have the honor of taking you for a short drive tomorrow?" he asked.

Prudence nodded. "I should like that."

"Good. May I take you out at the unfashionable hour of eleven o'clock?"

"I think I can manage to be up," she replied.

"Your servant, ladies." Brimley tipped his hat and trotted off.

Prudence's dreamy gaze followed his retreating figure.

"He is terribly handsome," whispered her sister. "I am sure kissing him would not be like kissing a prune."

Prudence feigned a shocked look and her sister giggled. They were still in high spirits when they returned home, and Aunt Louisa, seeing her niece suffered no ill effects from her outing, decided the doctor was right. Prudence was truly recovered and, yes, she could definitely plan on attending the Everly ball.

"The Everlys are richer than nabobs," Prudence told her sister later that night as they shared their customary purloined snack. "I should be able to find a trinket that will keep my orphans in comfort for some time."

Constance looked alarmed. "Surely you don't mean to keep this up any longer," she said.

"I mean to keep it up 'til the end of the season, at least. By then, I hope to find other means to help those poor unfortunates."

Constance looked anxious.

"I do not understand why you are so worried."

"Because not everyone is as stupid as you think. Someone is going to find you out. Please, dear, think of the scandal." Prudence was silent and Constance continued. "No matter how good the cause, you are still giving away money that does not belong to you. You are still stealing. The only difference between you and the pickpocket on the street is that you are better dressed."

Prudence's eyes filled with tears. She didn't know which hurt worse, her sister's words or the realization that Constance was right. "What a terrible thing to say," she cried.

Constance put both arms around her sister. "You must give up this dangerous game before it is too late," she said.

Prudence sniffed, although inwardly she was relieved. It was time to give up her double life. "All right," she said finally. "If this is preying on your mind so heavily I cannot in good conscience continue."

"I am so glad," breathed Constance.

A letter arrived from Mr. Biddle the next morning that made it impossible for Prudence to keep her promise. There had been a fire at the home. No lives were lost, but extensive damage had been done. The entire west wing was gone. He would not want to pressure Miss Pennhallow in any way, as she had already been so generous, but a disaster of this magnitude had not been provided for and there were some urgent needs. The board of trustees was calling an emergency meeting and surely things would work out eventually. But if she could spare a small donation it would be greatly appreciated at this time.

Prudence could not spare so much as a farthing at this time. But she knew of someone who could. Prudence bit her lip as her conscience sparred with this new dilemma. A promise is a promise, she thought. But surely Constance would not expect her to keep it under these circumstances.

Prudence paced the floor and her thoughts went back and forth as well. She had so wanted to give up this wicked double life. But now the need at the orphanage was even greater than ever. She sighed. Much as she wanted to, she couldn't cry off now—not when those poor children needed her so desperately. Surely she could manage one last time without getting caught.

Prudence crumpled the letter and threw it on the grate. Constance was going for a drive with Lord Wentworth. There was no sense upsetting her with news like this.

So Prudence very nobly refrained from spoiling her sister's drive. Although she certainly didn't do as much for Lord Brimley. The fair Miss Pennhallow was much distracted, hardly attending to anything he said. And by the time he brought her home, his lordship was much put out. He brought his horses to a halt and turned an irritated stare on his companion. "Miss Pennhallow!"

"Oh!" Prudence jumped. "I am so sorry. I was not attending."

"I strongly suspected as much," he replied with asperity.

"Oh, dear. You are vexed with me. I don't blame you. I have been very rude. It is just that I had such bad news this morning."

"I am sorry to hear it," his lordship said, his voice unfreezing slightly. "Your family?"

"Oh, no. But something awful just the same. One of my . . . my family's charities—the Edgar Timms Home for Orphaned Children has had a fire and much of the building has been destroyed. Naturally it is most upsetting."

"Naturally," agreed Brimley, becoming more friendly.

"My! I am keeping you here talking when I am sure you do not want your horses left standing like this," Prudence said. "I do apologize."

"Nonsense. I can certainly understand your worry—and share your concern." Brimley studied his companion's fair face. She had obviously left him again, her thoughts with the occupants of the orphanage. Her brow was wrinkled and her lips pursed. Not for the first time he had a sudden urge to kiss those full, red lips and see if they were really as soft as they looked. Instead he jumped down from the curricle and helped Prudence alight. "Don't worry about your orphans, Miss Pennhallow. I am sure they will receive the help they need," he said and made a mental note to have his man of business send the orphanage a sizable donation.

Instead of being cheered by this obvious hint regarding his generous nature, Lord Brimley's companion set her dainty jaw in a most determined manner. "They certainly will," she said, the light of battle in her eyes. They reached the door and Prudence thanked her companion for his kind services. "It was a lovely morning for a drive and you deserved a more entertaining companion."

"Nonsense," replied Brimley, slightly mollified. "It is always a pleasure to be with you, Miss Pennhallow. I will look forward to seeing you at the Everly ball. Your servant."

He bowed over her hand and returned to his curricle, smiling at his folly. Pleasure. Would that word describe his morning's outing with the fair Miss Pennhallow? Hardly. It was no pleasure to be ignored. In fact, it was downright irritating! But she had apologized so prettily. And coming in second to a collection of scruffy orphans said much for the lady's generous character. Brimley cracked his whip and his horses sprang forward, drawing him quickly down the street, nearly as quickly as Miss Pennhallow had captured his heart.

Meanwhile, Prudence had no sooner got in the door when her sister poked her head out of the drawing room. "You're finally back!" Constance exclaimed. "I have such news for you," she said, pulling her inside. She shut the door and whirled around, grinning. "Please congratulate the future Lady Wentworth," she announced.

"Oh, Constance!" Prudence flew to her sister and hugged her. "I am so happy for you, dearest. But when did this all come about?"

"This morning. We never went for our drive. He talked to Papa and then he asked me to marry him—in this very room," Constance finished in an awed tone.

"Oh, it is all too wonderful!" exclaimed Prudence.

Just then Aunt Louisa entered the room. "I see Constance has told you her news," she said. "What good fortune! And, Prudence love, I cannot help but feel you will be next."

"Oh, yes," Constance breathed. "Just think, two Pennhallow weddings before the year is out. How wonderful that would be! And I am so glad you have given up your dangerous pastime, Prudence," she added when the sisters were alone later. "Now I can truly enjoy the Everly ball."

Fortunately for Prudence her sister was too preoccupied to notice the guilty flush that stole across her face. "This will be the last performance," she promised herself.

And a brilliant performance it was, too. Miss Pennhallow was seen to be a little tottery, but that was to be expected since she was only just recovered from such a bad sprain. All but one were taken in and only because that one had happened to see her backstage preparations.

Mr. Daltry had an assignation with Miss Lansing at the end of the hall. He was lurking in the

shadows of a large potted palm awaiting the heiress when he saw another lady approach. Miss
Pennhallow! What the devil was she doing running around loose? Maybe the lady had an assignation herself. Daltry pressed himself against the
wall and observed her with interest.

Prudence looked quickly around her, then, to
Mr. Daltry's surprise, she lifted the skirt of her
gown and gave it a vigorous pull. There was a
ripping sound as flounce and skirt parted. Miss
Pennhallow quickly dropped the skirt back in
place and turned in the direction of the ballroom.

Mr. Daltry, puzzled by this bizarre behavior,
abandoned his post and followed Miss Pennhallow at a discreet distance. He stationed himself
inside the doorway and watched the dancers
gathering. Miss Pennhallow had been claimed
and they were taking their places in the set. The
music started and the dancers came to life. He
watched her carefully as she executed the move-
ments of the dance. And he watched, fascinated,
as she managed at just the right moment to insert
her gown under her partner's foot. The sound of
the rip was inaudible where he was, but he saw
the man's chagrin and couldn't help smiling to
himself as she consoled her partner. Clever girl!
What was she up to?

Mr. Daltry smiled and bowed as Miss Pennhallow exited the ballroom. He lingered at the door
only long enough for her to ascend the stairs,
then he followed. He reached the second floor in
time to see Miss Pennhallow enter a room at the
end of the hall. He padded after her. Success had

made her careless and she had not shut the door tightly. Daltry cracked it open and peeked in.

Thomas Daltry was an unscrupulous man, but even he was stunned at what he saw. Miss Pennhallow was calmly extracting an emerald bracelet from a jewel case. She held it up for inspection, then, for the second time that evening, gave Daltry a view of a nicely turned ankle as she raised her skirt. She propped her foot on a chair and quickly attached the bracelet to her leg. She then pulled a paper of pins from her reticule and proceeded to pin up her gown.

Daltry backed silently away and glided down the hall. So that is how her family managed so well, he thought. He had always had a hankering for the Pennhallow chit. She had a fire about her that most of these milk-and-water misses lacked. The more he thought about it, the more Daltry felt he had been wasting his time in pursuit of an heiress. He decided not to keep his rendezvous with Miss Lansing. She would wait. Right now another, more interesting scheme had presented itself.

Prudence returned to the ballroom unaware of the dark clouds gathering over her future. "My lord," she addressed Brimley as he swept her across the room in three-quarter time, "you are amazingly light on your feet."

"For such a big man," he finished.

Prudence blushed. "You are putting words in my mouth. That is not what I meant. I am, I confess, surprised to find you so skilled a dancer. If you have been living in retirement these last few years, how can you have become so accomplished?"

"You forget I have a very sociable sister. She has been at great pains to de-rusticate me."

"I think she has succeeded admirably."

"Only when it comes to outward appearances." His lordship laughed. "I suppose inside I have changed little. I am a simple man and definitely old-fashioned by today's standards. I still value a simple life marked by loyalty and honesty."

"Sir, there is not an Englishman who does not!"

Brimley raised an eyebrow at his partner and smiled. "Miss Pennhallow, we both know that in society things are not always as they seem. This room is filled with men and women who have played each other false since their wedding. Such duplicity and double-dealing are not for me."

Prudence gulped as the earl drew her closer. "I seek an honest heart, free from the disease of deception."

Her guilty heart raced. "Surely, sir, there is no such paragon in this world."

"I think there is," said Brimley softly.

This was too much and Prudence let out a sob.

"What is it? Have I said something to offend you?"

"No," she said. "I find my foot is paining me."

Her heart was paining her, too. And Prudence rode home that night with more than an emerald bracelet weighing her down. Misery came upon her like a fever and she slept poorly. But the missive that her abigail brought in the morning turned her misery into terror. She waited until

Lilly had closed the door behind her, then opened it. The words jumped off the page and grabbed her by the heart:

> *I know you for a thief. If you wish your secret to remain safe, meet me at Kensington Gardens, one o'clock.*

Chapter Seventeen

Prudence felt the blood run from her face. She sat staring at the letter and soon the writing began to swim as her eyes filled with tears. Oh, what a fool she had been! Constance had been right all along. If only she had listened to her sister. Someone must have discovered her the night before. She wiped her eyes and studied the letter again. It was no use. There was no clue either in the letter itself or on the envelope to tell her who had sent it. Lilly had remarked that the courier who brought it was a stranger. She shredded it and threw it on the grate.

She rang for Lilly. "It is going to be a nice day. I wish to go for a walk in Kensington Gardens. I would like you to accompany me."

"And Miss Constance?"

"We won't bother her."

Lilly looked at the scraps of paper on the grate and put two and two together, in this case getting five, concluding her mistress was meeting a lover. "Yes, miss," she said.

The spring flowers were in full bloom and if Prudence hadn't been so upset she would truly have enjoyed her early afternoon ramble. As it was, she parked Lilly on a bench and wandered up and down the paths, oblivious to the beauty around her.

"Good day, Miss Pennhallow," said a pleasant voice at her elbow. "Fancy running into you here."

"Oh!" Prudence jumped. "Mr. Daltry. This is a surprise."

"Why, yes," he said with a smile. "I am sure it is. Would you care to walk a little or are you . . . meeting someone?"

"I?" Prudence's laugh sounded artificial even in her own ears. "Fie on you, Mr. Daltry! No, it was such a fine day I thought I should like to come to the park."

"And your lovely sister, she does not share your interest in fauna and flora?"

"Oh yes, she does. But she is such a slugabed. I grew tired of waiting for her."

"So I do not detain you from anything or . . . anyone?"

"No. I assure you." Prudence was suddenly suspicious.

"Curious," he continued. "I am here to meet someone." She stiffened. He took her arm and steered her down a short path to a rustic bench. "The person I am here to meet is a very clever and accomplished young lady. She is very beautiful, too. And she bears a strong resemblance to you, Miss Pennhallow."

For the second time that day the blood drained from Prudence's face. She turned terrified eyes on Mr. Daltry.

"I always wondered how the Pennhallows managed so well on so little. If I'd only known of your talents, dear lady, I would never have dropped my suit."

Prudence blushed a deep scarlet. "I am sure I don't know what you mean," she said, her terrified heart racing.

A slow smile spread across Daltry's face. "Oh, but I am sure you do. What a clever woman you are, little Prudence. I may call you Prudence, may I?"

"You may not!"

"Come now, dearest. That is not way to treat a man who admires you so very much." He took her hand and she snatched it from him. Unoffended, he merely smiled. "Very smart to use the trick of tearing your gown and then blaming it on that poor fool. What a marvelous excuse to get into milady's sitting room and help yourself to her emeralds. You are quite the expert. Would I be far off if I were to guess you have been practicing these little deceptions for some time? And I suppose this explains those famous dizzy spells of yours, too."

Prudence looked away in an effort to hide the fear on her face and gripped the bench to keep from showing how her hands were beginning to shake.

"Ah, what genius," he sighed with genuine admiration.

"What do you want?" she hissed.

"I want to make a business arrangement, dear lady—my silence in exchange for your services."

"You cad!" Prudence spat the words. "You horrid, evil man. This is blackmail."

"Yes, I suppose it is. But then, there is not a very pretty word for what you have been doing, either, my dear."

"I never kept the jewels!" she whispered.

"I am sure you did not," Mr. Daltry agreed politely.

"I never kept any of the money, either."

"Of course not. You spent it!"

"Not on myself. Any money I . . . acquired . . . went for a truly noble cause."

"I see there is no false modesty in the Pennhallow family," he murmured.

Prudence ground her teeth.

"Come now. We are straying far from the subject. And while I enjoy your company and hope to enjoy more of it in the future, we must not sit here too long. We don't want tongues to wag, do we?"

"What do you want?"

"As I said, I want to exchange my silence for your services."

"Go on," said Prudence.

"The Lansing ball is coming up next week."

Prudence turned to him. "No!" she gasped.

"Oh yes. I realize her ladyship will most likely wear the famous Lansing rubies, but she has a diamond necklace which is equally admired."

Prudence started at him in horror. "The Lansing diamonds," she gasped. "I could not."

"Oh, but I think you could . . . to avoid bringing scandal upon your family," he sneered. "What would the ladies of the ton say if they were to discover they had taken a snake to their bosom? What, I wonder, would be their reaction when they found one of their brightest jewels was nothing more than a common thief."

Prudence recoiled from her tormentor, her mind reeling at the consequences of her folly. "I'm not a common thief," she sobbed.

"No," agreed Daltry, patting her hand. "You certainly are not. You are most uncommon. You have genius and style. Ah, but not everyone in society would see it that way. Now," he said, suddenly businesslike, "do we have a deal?"

She nodded miserably.

"Good. You may deliver the Lansing diamonds to me the day after the ball. We can meet right here."

"No," said Prudence stoutly. "I will not leave the Lansings' roof with that necklace in my possession. I will deliver it to you that night. We'll meet at midnight. In the library."

"Oh, very well," he agreed. "I shall vanish by the library window then."

"You must make me one promise." Prudence turned to face her blackmailer.

"May I remind you that you are hardly in a position to be making demands?" said Mr. Daltry sweetly.

"You must promise to leave Miss Lansing alone."

Daltry looked surprised. Then he chuckled. "The defender of the innocent, eh? I may do that. In fact, I may find that I prefer Prudence Pennhallow."

Prudence glowered at him. "That is no promise. In fact, that sounds like another threat."

"It is as much promise as I can give at the moment, dear lady. I never like to cut myself off completely from any opportunities. However, I do believe my beloved lacks the necessary courage to defy her mama and cast her lot with mine."

"So, having failed to steal Lady Lansing's daughter, you will settle for her jewels!"

"Now, now. Let us not quarrel, my lovely partner. I think it is time we parted company. I will see you next week. And do not fail me. That would be most unwise."

Mr. Daltry bowed over her hand and left her shivering in the sunshine. She sat for a few moments, trying to compose herself and finally gave up, finding a brisk walk more suited to her present emotional condition.

What to do, what to do? The question echoed with every step. How could she rob her friend? But how could she not? Perhaps Mr. Daltry was bluffing. But could she afford to take that chance? If Daltry exposed her she would be ruined. Her family would be disgraced, and Constance could forget about Lord Wentworth. She was ruined whichever way she turned, for Mr. Daltry would never be satisfied with one theft. He would demand more of her and she would sink deeper and deeper into a life of crime. And then there was a certain large gentleman. What would he think of her if he learned of her scandalous double life? Prudence resolutely swallowed the sudden lump in her throat. That didn't even bear thinking of.

Oh, where would it all end? Someday she was bound to be caught. Would they hang her on Tyburn Hill? Prudence's hand touched her throat. As if walking to the gallows, she made her way slowly back to the bench where her abigail was waiting.

"Are you all right, Miss Prudence?" the girl asked. "I was getting worried."

"I am fine," she lied. "Let us go home, Lilly. I think I have had enough fresh air for one day."

Prudence arrived home to find her sister and aunt in the hall, drawing on their gloves. "Where have you been?" Aunt Louisa demanded. "We were to go shopping this afternoon!"

Prudence put a hand to her forehead. "Oh, dear, I completely forgot. You two go on without me."

"But, dearest," protested Constance, "you are here now. You can easily come with us. We are going to visit that new linen draper in Oxford Street."

Prudence gave a distracted shake of the head. "No. I am sorry to be so difficult, but I am feeling rather fagged. I think I shall go lie down."

"You don't look at all well," said Aunt Louisa, removing her glove. "Let me feel your forehead. Well, you don't feel hot."

"No. I am not sick. But I am tired."

"You have probably overdone. If you do not

feel up to it, we can forgo the opera tonight and spend a quiet evening at home."

The thought of being at home under her aunt's observant eye was horrible indeed. Prudence rallied. "Heavens, no! A little rest and I shall be right as rain."

"Well, we'll be off then. See that you do rest while we are gone," Aunt Louisa ordered.

"I shall. Good-bye, darlings."

Prudence did go to her room, but rest was impossible. She was much too agitated to lie still. Instead she paced the floor, trying desperately to think of a way out of her tangle.

But no solution came and before she knew it Constance and Aunt Louisa had returned and she had to force herself to show an interest in their purchases. Then it was time for tea and to dress for supper. The day seemed an endless string of tortures. Prudence thought she would go mad from trying to smile her way through them.

She was thankful when they reached the opera house and the curtain finally went up, freeing her mind to wander miserably in search of a solution.

Too soon the curtain came down on the first act, and the Pennhallows had visitors knocking at their box—Lord Wentworth and Lord Alvaney. If Miss Pennhallow was suffering from great mental anguish, neither of these young men noticed. There was one man who would, however, and she hoped fervently she would not run into him before the next week.

Her hope was exploded the very next evening. Lord Brimley was at Almack's and had obviously been looking for her. He came forward as soon as she arrived with a warm greeting and an even warmer look. Prudence's lips trembled as she looked into those kind brown eyes and saw the happiness she could have had.

"Why, what kind of greeting is this?" his lordship teased. "Surely your aunt has not forbidden you to dance tonight!"

Prudence managed a watery chuckle. "Heavens, no. But I am sadly out of sorts. There. Now you have been warned. If I were you I would not solicit my hand for a single dance, for there is nothing worse than the company of a female who has fallen into the melancholy patch."

"I am not such a heartless man that I would leave a lady in such straits. May I solicit your hand for a dance? We shall see if we cannot bring you out of that melancholy patch."

Prudence did try to rally but couldn't. As she danced with Lord Brimley she felt as if fate was playing a very mean trick on her. She heartily wished she was just like all the other young ladies present at the ball. Their lives were quite ordinary and their futures bright. Hers looked stormy and threatening—and very, very lonely. Her smile never reached her eyes that evening. Her ready humor failed her and her laughter was forced.

"Can you not tell a good friend what troubles you so?" Brimley asked later, as he handed her a cup of lemonade.

Prudence yearned to confide in him, but instead she took a sip of lemonade. "Nothing troubles me, my lord, which I have not brought upon myself. It is a small matter. Pray, let us not talk about it. I should like to talk of something gay, if you please."

All evening Brimley watched her with a heavy heart. What ailed Miss Pennhallow? Probably her rakehell father was in another financial scrape. What a burden for such delicate shoulders to bear! He watched her sad attempt to be gay and his heart ached. He knew that as a friend he could do little to help her. And he suddenly longed to protect her, to be in a position to spare her any pain. There was only one way he could do that.

Brimley squared his shoulders. Did he love the woman or not? There was no longer any need to even ask such a question. Well, then, he lectured himself, surely he was brave enough to face whatever skeletons lurked in her family closet. And he had obviously better face them soon, for something was definitely wrong and he sensed she needed his help.

Chapter Eighteen

The next morning found Lord Brimley in the library of Pennhallow House, nervously awaiting Lord Pennhallow. "Well, well," said his lordship, ambling to his desk and indicating a chair for Brimley. "This is an early hour, so I gather you must be here on important business."

"I am sure you can guess what it may be, sir," said the earl.

"Yes, I see you have taken a fancy to my Prudence. A right good chess player, ain't she?"

Brimley smiled and nodded. "She is quite accomplished."

"Yes. Prudence ain't talented in the ordinary way, but she's head and shoulders above all these other milk-and-water misses. Takes after her mother. She was an unusual woman, too, my Mary." Pennhallow allowed his thoughts to drift and Brimley waited patiently. "Well," he said at last, towing himself back to the present, "you have my permission to speak. Of course, you know if you want my daughter, you'll most likely have to tow me out of the River Tick."

"I suspected as much, sir," Brimley said soberly.

While the gentlemen were settling her future, Prudence was already up and pacing her room. She had heard the door and knew Lord Brimley was closeted with her papa. That could mean only one thing. What could she do? What could she say? She couldn't say yes, but she hated to say no. Sending away her future happiness was a thought too horrible to be entertained. She knew that was what she must do eventually but, oh, not yet. She couldn't just yet, not with a horrible fate hanging over her. She could stall by asking for time to consider Lord Brimley's offer. But what would Auntie say if she did that? What possible reason could she give for hesitating to accept an offer that had been her sole objective for the last three weeks? No. The only answer was to avoid seeing Lord Brimley.

But what excuse could she give not to come downstairs when summoned? How could she avoid her suitor? There was only one thing to which a lady could resort—illness.

Prudence threw off her wrapper and ran to the washstand. She dipped her hands in the water pitcher and proceeded to dampen her forehead and hair, then her neck and nightgown. She threw open the window and leaned out, letting the crisp spring air chill her properly. Then, shivering, she closed the window, applied more water, and jumped into bed. And just in time.

There was a knock at the door and Aunt Louisa's head appeared. "Wonderful news!" she exclaimed. "You must get up, slugabed, for you shall never guess who is here to ask for your hand!"

Prudence moaned and turned her head.

"What is this?" exclaimed Aunt Louisa. "Oh, Prudence, you cannot be ill—not now!" She rushed to the bed and felt her niece's clammy forehead. "Oh, no," she moaned.

"A-A-Auntie," Prudence stammered through chattering teeth. "I am so c-c-c-cold."

"We must send for the doctor. You must get well immediately," wailed Aunt Louisa and she hurried from the room, leaving the door ajar in her haste.

The faint rustle of voices drifted up to Prudence and she closed her eyes and breathed a sigh of relief. He was gone for the moment. But how long could she keep this up? And what was the sense in it, really? She would have to tell the earl she could not marry him. Why torment herself by postponing it? Because Papa and Aunt Louisa would both be so angry when they heard and she knew she could not face them. No, she must put off Lord Brimley as long as possible.

She shut her door and crept to the water pitcher again. There was a soft knock and before she could do anything, her sister was in the room. "Prudence! What are you doing?"

"Shh," she hissed. "You must not say anything. Promise?"

"Of course I promise. Only tell me what you are doing?"

"I am pretending to be sick," Prudence explained.

"You must be mad," said her sister, astonished.

"Not yet, but I may be soon," Prudence said, crawling back into bed.

"I don't understand. Don't you want to marry Lord Brimley?"

"Oh yes, more than anything," Prudence wailed and pulled the bedclothes over her head and began to cry.

Before Constance could get any more out of her, Aunt Louisa had returned. "Constance dear, you must not be in the room with your sister so ill. I do not want you to catch this." She shooed her out of the room and returned to her niece's bedside. "There now," she soothed. "His lordship has promised to call again tomorrow."

This news did not have the desired effect. It only made the patient wail more loudly. "Oh, dear, I do hope this is not a fever of the brain," muttered Aunt Louisa.

Again the doctor came to examine Prudence. But her problem was not so easy to diagnose as the last time. For the life of him the doctor could not figure out what was wrong. "There is no fever, no swelling of the neck. Her pulse is a little rapid, but if she was as agitated as you described that would certainly account for a rapid pulse. The young lady appears to be merely overwrought. Does she have a nervous disposition?"

Aunt Louisa shook her head. "Heavens, no. The child has always had an easygoing nature."

"Something has obviously occurred which has strained her nerves. I would suggest a little laudanum to quiet her and complete bedrest for the next day or two."

Once again Prudence was sentenced to her bedchamber, this time in solitary confinement. For although Aunt Louisa had the greatest confidence in Dr. Swan, she was taking no chances and would allow Constance nowhere near the sickroom.

On the third day, however, after hearing Lord Brimley had been turned from the door, Prudence made a remarkable recovery. She got up and bathed and dressed and ventured as far as the drawing room. "I cannot feign illness forever. What is the sense in putting it off? I will have to tell Lord Brimley I cannot marry him."

"I do not understand," said Constance. "Why can you not marry Brimley?"

"Because I have been found out." Prudence turned tearfully to her sister.

Constance blanched and grabbed the arm of her chair. "No!"

Prudence nodded. "Yes. You warned me so many times. Oh, dearest and wisest of sisters, why didn't I listen to you? Now it is too late. I am known for a thief."

Constance sank back into her chair.

Prudence sighed. "And that is not the worst. The one who found me out is none other than Mr. Daltry. And he . . ." She paused, pressing her forehead into her hand, trying to gain control of her trembling voice. Finally she continued. "He is blackmailing me."

"No!"

"I am to steal the Lansing diamonds next week and deliver them to him in the library at midnight or he will expose me."

Constance gave a cry and her hand flew to her mouth. "Oh, surely he wouldn't."

"I am sure he would," said Prudence dully. "So you see, I cannot accept Lord Brimley's offer."

"But he loves you. Maybe he could help . . ."

"No," she sobbed. "He loves a girl who is frank and honest. He told me as much. He could not love an evil creature who has so wickedly deceived society."

Silence fell, broken only by an occasional sniff from Prudence. The girls remained so for several minutes until Aunt Louisa found them.

"Ah, here you are. Prudence, my love, it is good to see you up, although I must say you still look a little peaked. Constance, are you all right?" she asked, suddenly alarmed at seeing yet another drooping countenance.

Constance revived instantly. "Yes, I am fine, Auntie. May I have the landaulet this afternoon? I had thought to pay a call on Miss Lansing."

"I do not need it," said Aunt Louisa. "Although I think perhaps later we will take a drive. A little fresh air might put the bloom back in Prudence's cheeks."

Prudence felt sure nothing would ever restore her bloom, but she kept that thought to herself.

"You may rest upon the sofa this afternoon and after Constance returns we will all go for a drive. How does that sound?"

"That sounds fine," said Prudence weakly.

Her aunt gave her a worried look, then with forced cheerfulness said, "Good. That settles it. If you should need me for anything, I will be with Cook going over the menus for next week."

Aunt Louisa left and Constance ran to get her gloves and hat, leaving Prudence to brood alone. It was most unkind, she thought, of her sister to go gadding off when she was caught in such a tragedy. In fact, it was very unlike Constance to be so selfish.

Meanwhile, Constance had ordered the carriage brought round and was instructing her coachman. "To Farnsworth House," she said and sat back against the squabs, trying to calm her wildly bumping heart. She realized she was taking a chance in confiding in Angella. But the Pennhallow sisters had found a kindred soul in Lord Brimley's dashing sister. Somehow Constance knew she would understand their predicament and possibly even be able to make her brother understand. Surely he wouldn't mind so very much when he learned why Prudence had been stealing jewelry all season. And he would know what to do to rescue her from the evil Mr. Daltry.

Angella had been about to go out, but laid aside her gloves and invited Miss Pennhallow in. "How is your sister?" she asked. "My brother tells me she has been very ill."

"She is suffering greatly. And if we may be quite alone, I should like to tell you about it."

There was no mistaking the urgency in Miss Pennhallow's voice.

"Do be seated and tell me all about it," Angella ordered.

It was a long and rather disjointed story and by the time Constance was through, each lady was holding a very damp handkerchief. "This is dreadful," Angella said. She sighed and shook her head. "I have suspected her of being up to something these many weeks past, but I never dreamed she was involved in anything so . . . so . . ."

"Mad," sighed Constance.

Angella blushed. "Well, I can see that she had the purest of motives. But oh, dear, no one else will see that if word of this gets out, especially the ladies from whom she has stolen."

"What can we do?" asked Constance.

"I honestly don't know. We had better send for Brimley at once."

"Oh, dear," moaned Constance. "Prudence does not want him to know. She would rather suffer the worst imaginable fate than have him find out and think poorly of her. She loves him so."

Angella sighed. "It cannot be helped," she said finally. "We must have help and Brimley will know what to do. At least I hope he will, for I must confess I am at a standstill."

Chapter Nineteen

While the ladies awaited Lord Brimley, the cause of all their troubles was entertaining a visitor of his own.

"I been patient long enough, Daltry. You can hand over the blunt now or I spill your blood. Which will it be?"

"Neither," he replied calmly. "I am about to come into a very large sum of money."

"I've heard that before," his visitor growled.

Daltry chuckled. "Oh, but this time. . . It is too rich. If I thought you would understand all the subtleties, I would share the jest with you. Suffice it to say that by Monday next I will have in my possession a diamond necklace worth several thousand pounds. And that," he said, poking the man in the chest, "is just the beginning."

The man's eyes widened and he rubbed his stubbled chin. "Well. . . I'll give you to Monday then."

Daltry had no sooner gotten rid of his visitor

when there was another knock on the door. A minute later his man came in bearing a perfumed note. As he read the missive, Daltry's smile grew. He crumpled the letter and laughed out loud. "This is my lucky day. Devers!" he bellowed. The smirking valet reappeared. "Lay out my russet coat and my buff breeches. I have an appointment this afternoon in . . ." He checked his watch. "One hour. I shall have to hurry."

Mr. Daltry normally would have spent more time on his cravat, but after three tries he looked critically in his mirror and said, "It will have to do." Devers helped him into his coat and boots. He grabbed his walking cane and stepped out the door. In a few minutes he had found a hack and was on his way to Hookam's library.

An agitated Miss Lansing had nearly given him up and cried tears of joy when she saw him. She would have jumped up from the table where she sat and rushed to him if he had not frowned and shook his head slightly. She sank back down, blushing.

He sauntered to her table and sat down next to her. "What is it, my love?" he whispered. "I came as quickly as I could."

Elyza lowered her eyes. "You never came."

"But I am here," he objected.

"No. The other night . . ."

"Oh, but I did." Daltry recalled the lucky circumstance of being hidden from Miss Pennhallow behind the potted palm. "I waited and you did not show, so I was sure you had been trifling with me all along."

"Oh, no," declared Elyza. "I would never do

such a thing." She put a timid hand on his arm. "I am in terrible trouble. You see, Mr. Bexton has asked for my papa's permission to marry me. And Mama has as good as ordered me to accept," she ended on a sob.

"There now. Don't cry," Daltry soothed, patting her hand. "We shall think of something."

"There is no time," she whispered. "We must *do* something."

He sighed, giving a good imitation of a man with his back to the wall. "Then there is only one thing we can do. We must fly to the border."

Elyza's eyes shone up at him.

"This is a terrible thing to ask of you, my dear. But I see no other way. Can you stall Mr. Bexton until after your mama's ball? After all, there is no sense in upsetting her any more than necessary. Bad enough to elope, but to ruin her ball on top of that . . ."

"Oh, you are right," agreed Elyza. "I am sure I can put Bexton off for a few days."

"Then we shall fly that very night. No. Better yet, we shall leave on Monday, early in the morning. Can you slip away?"

"I think so," she whispered.

"Good. Bring only a portmanteau with you. I shall be waiting on the corner with a carriage at half past seven."

Elyza nodded.

"Oh, and dearest . . ."

"Yes?"

"Bring any jewels you have. We may stand in need of them."

Elyza nodded.

"I hate to do this," whispered her lover. "To expose you to such scandal."

"We can survive a little scandal," said Elyza naively. "Besides, Papa and Mama have forced us to this." She was silent for a moment. "Once it is done, they will surely forgive us," she said tentatively.

Daltry was sure of that himself. He smiled at his own cleverness. "Yes, my love. They will. Until Monday," he said. "No. Until Saturday. Save me a waltz, dearest one." And on that parting speech he made his exit, leaving the library just as Brimley, on the other side of town, was entering his sister's drawing room.

"Angel. What is the urgent matter that requires my immediate assistance?" he asked. His smile froze when he saw her guest. "Miss Pennhallow, your servant."

"It is about Prudence," said Angella. "You had better sit down."

"I will stand, thank you. Tell me quickly. Is she worse?"

"My sister was never ill. Well, not in body. But she has been sick at heart for days. Oh, your lordship, she is in such trouble!" Constance began to sob.

"Here now," Brimley said, offering her his handkerchief. "I cannot help if you do not tell me what the trouble is. Do try to be brave, Miss Pennhallow."

But Constance had used up all her courage and now all she could do was cry. Brimley looked desperately at his sister.

Angella swallowed hard. "Prudence is being blackmailed."

"Blackmailed!" he bellowed. His sister gave him a quelling look and he lowered his voice. "Whatever can the girl have done? Is it because of something Lord Pennhallow has done?"

Angella shook her head, finding the situation suddenly very difficult to explain.

"Well, what then?" cried his lordship, growing exasperated.

"She . . . he . . . that is . . ." Angella stammered to a halt. She tried again. "Mr. Daltry saw her take . . . something and now he is threatening to expose her."

"What did she take?" asked Brimley, still uncomprehending.

"She took Lady Everly's emerald bracelet," wailed Constance.

"My God." Brimley dropped into the nearest chair.

"He is forcing her to steal Lady Lansing's diamond necklace and deliver it to him at the Lansings' ball," continued Constance. His lordship stared at her uncomprehendingly. Constance closed her eyes, took a deep breath, and plunged on. "You see, it all started because she wanted to help the poor, like our Aunt Louisa does. Aunt Louisa is very generous in her contributions to charity, you see."

His lordship nodded, his face a mask.

"Well, one day we were talking about Prudence's desire to help others. And I . . . I said, 'Why don't you do like Robin Hood and rob from the rich and give to the poor.' I only said it in jest, but Prudence thought it was an excellent idea and . . . and that is how it all started. So you see, it is all my fault." Constance ended on a wail and descended again into her hankie. She resurfaced after a refreshing cry. "Prudence never kept any of the money she got for the jewels. She gave it to the Edgar Timms Home for Orphaned Children."

"How many times did she stea . . . do this?" asked Angella.

Constance screwed up her face in concentration. "Let me see. There was Lady Ames, Lady Sorenson, and Lady Ludlow and Lady Everly and oh, I cannot remember. Perhaps one other."

"That is not too awfully many," said Angella thoughtfully.

"And she still has Lady Everly's emerald bracelet," put in Constance.

"What do you think?" Angella asked Brimley. "Can we not do something to help her?"

Constance looked into those suddenly cold eyes and her heart sank. "I . . . shouldn't have come," she said. "Prudence did not want you to know. She is prepared to do Mr. Daltry's bidding rather than bring scandal on her family or involve either of you in any way." Still Lord Brimley did not speak. "I think I had better get back," she said and rose slowly.

"Don't worry," said Angella, walking her to the door. "We shall think of something."

But Constance had seen Lord Brimley's face. She knew they could expect no help from that quarter. "You are very kind," she murmured. "At any rate, I know you will keep our secret. Good day."

Angella came back to the drawing room and shut the door. "Well?" she asked.

"Well what?" replied her brother.

"Don't fence with me, Eddie. What are we going to do to help the girl?"

"I don't see what we can do," said her brother calmly. "She will have to suffer the consequences of her actions."

Angella's mouth dropped. "I cannot believe I am hearing this," she said. "Do you know that that man is using her to steal the Lansing diamonds! If she does not, he has threatened her with exposure." Her brother remained silent. "Don't you understand?"

"I understand perfectly," said Brimley, his voice rising. "I understand that this woman was not at all what she seemed. She has used me and every other fool in London as her tool! What a fool I was!"

"You! All you can think about is yourself, your feelings, your wounded pride? Yes, she did a foolish thing, the poor misguided girl. But her feelings for you were genuine. Anyone with half a wit could see that. And even now, as she is suffering such anguish, she thinks of sparing your feelings. Oh, you do not deserve her!" Angella turned in disgust and headed for the door. "Don't help her then. Her sister and I will think of something. You may let yourself out, Edward. And the sooner the better!" With that parting shot, Angella flounced from the room, leaving her brother staring after her.

Chapter Twenty

The day of the Lansing ball was as gray as Prudence's spirits. She looked out her bedroom window and sighed, wishing she could stay in that cozy chamber all day. But alas, her fate awaited her.

A letter had been brought round the day before from Angella telling Prudence not to despair, for she was sure she would come up with a plan to rescue her. "What does this mean?" Prudence had asked her sister. "Does Brimley know?" Constance hung her head. "You told him. Constance, how could you?"

"We were in need of help. I thought surely if I explained, he would come through since he loves you so."

Prudence had thrown herself on her bed and cried bitterly. "Not a word," she sobbed. "We have not heard a word. Now he knows all and he does not love me anymore. Why did you tell him? You could have at least spared me that grief."

Now the day of the ball had come and Prudence stared at the leaden skies with a heavy heart. She turned at the sound of a gentle tap on her door. Constance entered and Prudence tried to give her a smile.

"How are you?" she asked.

"I am ready," said Prudence. "I just wish I did not have this endless day to get through."

"Let us go downstairs and eat something. Then perhaps a shopping expedition would . . ."

"Shopping!" interrupted Prudence. "Oh, how can I think of shopping at a time like this?"

But something had to be done to fill the hours and shopping turned out to be a good distraction for Prudence. The lure of the modistes and milliners was more than any young lady could resist and Prudence decided if she was going to be hanged for a thief she may as well ride to Tyburn Hill fashionably dressed.

The sisters managed to use up the better part of the day investing in their appearance. More time was spent when they arrived home in showing Aunt Louisa their purchases and discussing the merits of each bonnet, shawl, and glove. By the time this was done tea was ready. And before Prudence knew it she was dressing for dinner. The day that had begun so slowly had now sped up, bringing her closer and closer to that dreadful moment when she must begin her life of crime.

She was unusually quiet as they sat in the long line of carriages waiting to disgorge their fashionable passengers at the Lansing door. "You are quiet tonight, child," said Aunt Louisa. "Are you not feeling quite the thing?"

"She is probably wondering what she will say to a certain someone," teased Pennhallow. "I'll lay odds he won't wait beyond this night to speak. By God, you look pretty enough to carry off!"

This little speech brought only tears and Prudence turned her head toward the window, suddenly interested in the crowd ogling the procession of carriages.

"Don't tease her, Harold. She is nervous enough as it is," scolded Aunt Louisa. "You do look very lovely tonight, dear," she continued in softer accents. "That light pink becomes you. I do wish you had a little more color. You still look pale."

Prudence wished she had a little more time. Suddenly things were moving too fast. She waited in line to greet her hostess with a wildly thumping heart.

Elyza was standing between her parents and when Prudence stopped to shake her hand she leaned over and whispered, "I have such wonderful news for you!" Prudence's eyes widened in alarm. Miss Lansing mistook her look for surprise and nodded excitedly, then passed Prudence on to her papa.

"Oh, dear, this on top of everything else," she moaned as she and Constance entered the ballroom. "Let us hope it is not tonight for that will be truly more than I can bear."

Lord Wentworth's arrival ended this conversation, as he insisted on bearing Constance off to greet his mama. Prudence smiled wistfully after them. Above all, she must not jeopardize her sister's chances for such a brilliant match.

In vain she searched the crowded room, but there was no sign of Lord Brimley.

Aunt Louisa had already found a crony to gossip with and was comfortably planted in a gilt chair for the night. Prudence was about to join her when a rustle of silk at her elbow made her turn. A gloved hand caught her arm and Angella came into view, her face framed in brown curls. "Hello," she whispered, "how are you holding up?"

"Not very well," Prudence admitted.

"Come help me adjust my gown. I have a plan."

The two women disappeared into the anteroom reserved for ladies' wraps. "I am going to help you frame Daltry," Angella whispered, shutting the door. "When are you to deliver the necklace and where?"

"In the library at midnight."

"Very well. I will wait until five minutes past. Then I shall burst in on you and scream at the top of my lungs. Naturally, people will come rushing . . . I hope. Well, I am sure someone will hear. Anyway, I shall say I saw Mr. Daltry coming from a direction of the house where I felt he had no business. I followed him down the hall where I saw him accost you and push you into the library. I followed and found him forcing himself on you. You say that he had been drinking too much and was trying to force you to fly with him and that he told you he had taken something which would allow the two of you to live well for some time. Just make sure he has the necklace in his coat pocket or *somewhere* on his person."

The door opened at that moment and there was no time for questions. Angella was again a gay young matron preparing to enjoy herself at the ball. Prudence followed her lead and the two women smiled at the newcomer and left the room chatting amiably, Angella suddenly anxious to tell Prudence all about the loo party she had attended the day before.

As the evening progressed it took on a nightmarish quality. Mr. Daltry had the nerve to solicit Prudence's hand for a waltz, which she politely refused. He smiled as if at some secret joke, bowed, and left. The rest of the evening she caught glimpses of him watching her. Every time their eyes met he smiled that horrid smile and bowed. She finally saw Brimley, but he made no move in her direction, choosing instead to dance with every wallflower in the room. Prudence sighed.

Finally, she could delay no longer. The unfortunate Mr. Smythe was, again, her tool and she nearly bore him to the ground when she slumped against him in the middle of the waltz. He looked in vain for her aunt or sister, but they had removed to the far end of the room and did not see his predicament.

Prudence did not want to make a large scene, so she revived almost instantly and was able, with help, to walk off the dance floor. "I fear I gave you an awful fright," she murmured.

"You certainly did!" agreed Mr. Smythe. "Nearly knocked us both over," he continued, forgetting his manners. "Here now, let's get you somewhere that you can lie down. Oh, good," he said. "There is her ladyship now."

Ten minutes later Prudence found herself reposing in her hostess's sumptuous bedroom. Her ladyship would have stayed with her, but Prudence insisted she return to her guests.

"Then I shall send your aunt to you," said
Lady Lansing.

"Oh, pray do not," begged Prudence. "I do not
wish to bother Auntie."

"Nonsense, child. She is here to watch over
you and she would be most distressed if I did not
fetch her, let me assure you."

Prudence sighed and leaned back against the
pillows. It was useless to resist. "Perhaps you are
right," she said.

"Of course I am," said Lady Lansing, patting
her arm. "You just rest and I shall send your aunt
up directly."

"Thank you," said the invalid.

The door had barely closed when Prudence
bounded up. Oh, what a horrid complication! As
if she didn't have enough to worry about. What
she would do if her aunt were to find her, she had
no idea. "Hurry, hurry," she muttered and
quickly began her search. She almost hoped she
would not find the necklace. Surely something so
valuable would be locked away.

Unfortunately, it was not. She found it in a
case in her ladyship's wardrobe. The case was
locked, but Prudence had become so experienced
that the lock was dealt with in a matter of seconds. She opened the lid and her heart sank as
the famous Lansing diamonds twinkled up at her.
She lifted the piece with a shaking hand. There
was no mistaking that famous necklace—a cluster
of diamonds set in silver and worked together in
a delicate sparkling web. The craftsmanship was
exquisite. Looking at it, the horror of what she
was doing, and had been doing all season, hit

Prudence. Whatever had driven her to such madness?

She tightened her fist around the necklace in sudden determination. This necklace must not fall into Mr. Daltry's hands. Angella's plan *must* work!

Remembering the need for haste, Prudence dashed to the door. She peered out. Too late! Auntie was already coming down the hall. Prudence looked around for a place to hide. Under the bed? No. Auntie might look there. The curtains? They were just far enough from the bed that they might not come into Auntie's field of vision. And if she stood very still . . . Prudence pulled aside the long curtains and stepped in back of them, willing her galloping heart to slow down.

The door opened and Aunt Louisa rushed in. She halted after three steps, looking at the bed, her mouth gaping "Prudence!" she called. She bent and looked under the bed and then stood up, looking perplexed. "Drat the girl!" she exclaimed and marched from the room.

Prudence waited a few seconds to make sure her aunt wouldn't return, then tiptoed to the door. The hall was empty and she crossed it and ran lightly down the stairs. She reached the library nearly undetected. As she opened the door the mantel clock was striking the hour.

The figure seated at the desk stood up. "Twelve o'clock exactly. Punctuality is a rare virtue, Miss Pennhallow."

Prudence stood for a moment, unable to move, and watched as Daltry walked around and seated himself comfortably on the desktop. "I believe you have something for me?" he said at last.

Quickly she brought out the necklace and handed it over. He held it up, watching the light dance and sparkle on the stones. So involved was he in admiring his prize that he didn't hear the door softly open.

"Miss Pennhallow, your aunt is looking for—" Miss Lansing stopped just inside the door. "Mr. Daltry, Thomas! What are you doing? What have you . . . ?"

"I believe he has your mama's necklace," came a voice behind her.

"Oh, Lord Brimley," gasped Prudence.

Daltry looked wildly around, then suddenly grabbed a letter opener from the desk. "Don't come a step closer," he said, locking his arm across Prudence's shoulders.

At that moment Prudence's eyelids fluttered and she slumped down, suddenly becoming dead weight in her captor's arms and throwing him off balance.

Miss Lansing screamed as Brimley ran past her and leapt at Daltry. The three went down in a tangle of legs and skirt.

"Prudence, you can stop pretending—get out of the way," Brimley shouted as the two men struggled for each other's throats. But Prudence didn't move. For the first time in her life she had really fainted.

The battle was brought to a quick and ignoble end with the arrival of Angella, Lady Lansing, and Constance close behind her.

"Stop this immediately!" Lady Lansing commanded and the two men scrambled to their feet. The necklace lay glittering on the floor. Brimley scooped it up and presented it to Lady Lansing.

"I am afraid we have all given our trust to someone unworthy of it," he said. His sister's eyes widened and Constance gulped. Prudence said nothing but still lay inert on the floor, oblivious of impending doom. "This person," Brimley said, pointing at Daltry, "is a thief."

"That is true," said Angella. "I saw him skulking in the hall just a few minutes ago and I saw something glittering in his hand."

Lady Lansing's considerable chest heaved. "For your mama's sake we befriended you," she said. "And you have betrayed that friendship. It is only for your mama's sake that we will not now take legal action against you. But you are no longer welcome here. And I shall see to it you are not welcome anywhere in London. Now leave my home."

Daltry glared at Brimley, then stormed from the room.

"What will become of him?" sobbed Elyza.

"He will most likely flee to the Continent where one would hope he will mend his ways. Come, child, we have guests."

"But Miss Pennhallow . . ."

"Is in good hands," replied Lady Lansing as the earl lifted Prudence tenderly in his arms.

"I think we are not wanted," Angella whispered to Constance, and they followed the Lansings, shutting the door softly behind them.

The insistent slapping of her face brought Prudence back to consciousness. "Oh, mercy," she moaned. "Do stop it. Oh, Lord Brimley."

"I prefer Edward," said the earl.

"I am so ashamed. You know all, don't you?"

"Yes, my little Robin Hood. I am afraid I do."

"I was so wicked," Prudence sobbed, turning her face into his lordship's coat.

"No," said Brimley, stroking her hair. "Not so much wicked as misguided. From now on we need to find safer avenues for you to pursue your love of adventure. And more, um, conventional means for your philanthropies."

Prudence, pricked to the heart, only sobbed louder.

"In fact, I think I have found a scheme whereby we can do that."

Prudence sniffed and looked at him, then shook her head. "Please, no more schemes for me."

"But I think you will like this one," he insisted. "Marry me."

"Marry you?" she repeated stupidly.

"I have a fair fortune with which you can be as philanthropic as you wish and if you are still desirous of adventure, we can travel."

For a moment, Prudence indulged herself with a vision of the happy future she could have had. One last tear fell as she firmly shut the door on that pleasant vision. She loved Lord Brimley too much to risk his future happiness on such a havey-cavey girl as herself. She shook her head and scrambled to her feet. "No, no. Please do not ask me again. Ever!" Her voice broke on a sob and she rushed from the room, leaving him puzzled and angry.

Angella and Constance had been hovering in the hall with their congratulations and best wishes ready, but the sight of a distressed Prudence fleeing the room caused them to stare at each other in bewilderment.

While Constance rushed after her sister, Angella ventured back into the library. She shut the door softly and stood watching her brother pace the floor.

"She refused me!" he wailed.

"Edward, shh," she cautioned.

Brimley compressed his lips and resumed his pacing. But it wasn't long before he began to rave again. "How could she do such a thing? To engage my heart and then so callously cast me away. The girl has no heart. Well, I am glad I found out before it was too late. I tell you this, Angel, I'm going back to Fairhaven tomorrow. I have had quite enough of town life."

Angella watched her brother calmly as he continued to seethe. He finally stopped and looked at her haughtily. "I am making a fool of myself, aren't I?"

She nodded.

Brimley took a deep breath and looked to a far corner of the room. "What have you to say for your sex, dear sister?"

"Nothing," Angella calmly replied. "But I think I might safely say something on behalf of Miss Pennhallow."

Brimley stood like a statue. "I am listening," he said.

"She refuses you because she loves you."

"That is foolish," he snapped.

"I fear so," admitted his sister. "But I suspect she fears her escapades will now be found out and she would keep you from sharing her shame."

"No!" exclaimed Brimley, thunderstruck. "Do you really think so? The poor, darling girl. But it makes perfect sense. Of course that is exactly how she would think. I will go find her immediately."

Angella stepped quickly aside as her brother rushed past her and out the door. How undignified Eddie was behaving. How she would roast him. "I suppose we must now make that dinner an engagement celebration," she said to herself.

She emerged from the library only to see her brother angrily smashing his chapeau bras on his head. Once again he looked like a thundercloud. "Oh, dear, what now," she muttered. "Edward?"

"She has gone home," he said through clenched teeth. "A pox on all females and good night."

Chapter Twenty-one

Lord Brimley pulled his curricle up to the Pennhallows' town house. His scowl gave him the appearance of a man about to give someone a lashing, but in truth he had come to propose marriage. Who would ever have thought a sensible man such as he would be doing such a foolish, impractical thing. Why propose to a woman who had already refused him? He should thank God for his narrow escape and get out of town. After all, it was becoming quite plain that she was mad, queer in her attic. What kind of children would she produce? What did it matter? He loved her and he wanted her. And he would have her! Brimley ran up the steps and banged the knocker loudly.

The butler looked dismayed at the sight of him, but Brimley was too full of his own thoughts to notice it. "Please inform Miss Pennhallow that I wish to see her," he said, handing Ames his hat and gloves.

"Very good, sir, but . . ." Ames broke off. "If your lordship would care to wait in the drawing room, I will send someone to you directly."

Brimley thought this remark strange, but he did as he was bid and entered the drawing room. He didn't have long to wait. Aunt Louisa came in, wringing her hands. "Lord Brimley, this is a pleasant surprise," she said.

"I can see that," he replied, surveying the older woman's distraught face. "May I see your niece?"

"No! I mean, that is to say . . . she's not here at this moment." Aunt Louisa looked about the library as though searching for the missing person. She looked almost relieved when Constance joined them. "Perhaps you would like to call again tomorrow."

"I'll wait," said Brimley, calmly seating himself and crossing his legs.

"Well, you can't!" snapped Aunt Louisa. Then, remembering her manners, she began again in a more normal tone. "You see, she was called away suddenly and I have no idea when she will return and . . ."

"Oh, Auntie!" exclaimed Constance, "pray do stop beating about the bush and tell him."

"Tell me what?" asked Brimley.

"Prudence has gone."

"Gone?" he repeated.

"She's run away."

"What!" Brimley jumped from his seat. "Where has she gone?"

"To the orphanage. We found the note only an hour ago and we have sent James to find Papa . . ." Constance didn't finish her sentence. There was little point in finishing it, for the earl had already bolted from the room and was on his way out the front door.

An hour later he had found the Edgar Timms Home for Orphaned Children, or what was left of it, and was being ushered into a small, book-lined office. The acrid smell of smoke was pervasive, but Lord Brimley, normally very fastidious, did not notice it.

Mr. Biddle looked at his large, angry guest, took out his handkerchief, and mopped his bald pate.

"I am Lord Brimley," the giant announced, "and I have come to take Miss Pennhallow home."

"Yes, of course, sir," Mr. Biddle said in his high voice. He rubbed his hands together nervously. "I was sure someone would be coming for her. But she was so insistent on staying. Said she wanted to remain here and care for the children. Said she wanted to help supervise the rebuilding of the east wing. My letter must have upset her. She has been such a generous benefactress, naturally I felt she would want to know of our misfortune. But I never dreamed she would do something like this, I assure you, my lord."

His lordship's voice settled into kinder tones. "I understand. But naturally this will not do."

"Oh, me, no," agreed Mr. Biddle. "I shall fetch her."

"No," said Brimley. "I should like to surprise her. Can you tell me where she is?"

"I believe she is in the garden, sir, playing with the children. If your lordship will follow me."

Brimley nodded and followed the little man down a long hall and to the back of the large, rambling house. Mr. Biddle opened a door for him and he stepped out.

The sight that met him was enough to melt any heart. There, holding hands with a circle of squealing children and skipping in a circle, was

Miss Prudence Pennhallow. Her face was flushed
and she was laughing. Brimley smiled.

The children one by one saw him and the circle
came to a bumpy and rather somber halt. Prudence turned her head. Her smile died and her
eyes flew open wide.

Brimley walked down the steps and strolled
over to the circle. "May I?" he asked.

The children looked at him suspiciously, but
two of the older ones made a space for him and
gave him their hands.

"All right," said Prudence with forced gaiety.
"Let us try it again, shall we? Ring around the
rosey, pockets full of posies. Ashes, ashes, we all
fall down."

The children ended their song and fell, laughing, to the ground. Their laughter doubled at the
sight of the fine gentleman sitting on the ground
with them. Brimley got up and dusted his
breeches. "That was fun," he lied. "But now I
need to talk to your playmate. Miss Pennhallow?" He held out a hand to Prudence in a manner that brooked no argument.

Prudence rose, looking nervously at his lordship.

"I've come to take you home," he said as he led
her away from the children.

"I won't go," she replied stubbornly.

"And why not?"

"Because."

"That is hardly a satisfactory answer," said
Brimley.

"It is all the answer I am prepared to give, my
lord," she replied stiffly.

"Don't you think you could do your orphans more good as the wife of one of the richest men in England?" asked Brimley.

Prudence raised startled blue eyes to his.

"Marry me," he demanded.

"But I cannot."

"You must, you know, for I have grown quite fond of you."

"Oh, you dear man." Prudence sounded wistful. "I will cherish what you have said until my dying day."

"That's nice," said Brimley, drawing her hand through his arm and propelling her back toward the half-charred building.

"But I cannot marry you," she protested.

"Oh, but you can."

"No. You do not understand. The jewels—I was a thief!"

"As your career was a short one—only this season, I understand, I am sure I will be able to ransom the jewels you, er, disposed of. And I daresay you will find equally as many ingenious ways of returning them," said Brimley, steering his beloved through the door. "Now, while you are gathering your things, I will talk business with Mr. Biddle. Then I am taking you straight home, for you have a dinner party to attend tonight."

Prudence looked at Lord Brimley questioningly.

"At my sister's—it is to celebrate our betrothal. How would it look if I attended without my betrothed? Would you have me suffer such disgrace?"

"Oh, pooh." Prudence laughed as her eyes filled with tears. "You are impossible to resist. I only hope someday when you are sorry you acted so rashly you will remember I gave you a chance to escape."

Brimley's arm circled her waist and he drew her to him. "I have never acted more wisely." Then the earl did what he had been wanting to do ever since he first set eyes on Miss Prudence Pennhallow. And Prudence was delighted to discover that kissing Lord Brimley was not at all like kissing a prune.

A Message To Our Readers...

As a person who reads books, you have access to countless possibilities for information and delight.

The world at your fingertips.

Millions of kids don't.

They don't because they can't read. Or won't. They've never found out how much fun reading can be. Many young people never open a book outside of school, much less finish one.

Think of what they're missing—all the books you loved as a child, all those you've enjoyed and learned from as an adult.

That's why there's RIF. For twenty years, Reading is Fundamental (RIF) has been helping community organizations help kids discover the fun of reading.

RIF's nationwide program of local projects makes it possible for young people to choose books that become theirs to keep. And, RIF activities motivate kids, so that they *want* to read.

To find out how RIF can help in your community or even in your own home, write to:

RIF
Dept. BK-2
Box 23444
Washington, D.C.
20026

Founded in 1966, RIF is a national nonprofit organization with local projects run by volunteers in every state of the union.

REGENCY
ROMANTIC INTRIGUE
FROM PAGEANT BOOKS!

THE MAGNIFICENT MIRABELLE

Lydia Lee

Introducing twins with a talent for
intrigue! Neither Viola nor Mirabelle
wants to fall victim to the dictates of
their eccentric grandfather's will, so
together they join forces to ensure the
family fortune. From London's stately
homes to a rather unorthodox con-
vent, the sisters pursue thieves, fortunes, and their hearts' desires to a
deliciously satisfying conclusion.

ISBN: 0-517-00739-8   PRICE: $2.50

ON SALE NOW!